Crossing
Boarders

Happy Reading!

Debra Swift

Crossing Boarders

A Novel

Debra Sue Brice

Dove
Publishers

Dove Christian Publishers
P.O. Box 611
Bladensburg, MD 20710-0611
www.dovechristianpublishers.com

ISBN: 978-0-9903979-4-6

Published in the United States of America

Crossing Boarders is a work of fiction. Names, characters, places and incidents are the products of the author's imagination or are used fictitiously. Any resemblance to actual events, locales, or persions, living or dead, is entirely coincidental.

Book design by Raenita Wiggins
Cover photograph by Debra Sue Brice

To my mom, dad, and sister for always
having faith in me.

Chapter One

The bright, northern Ohio sun was just starting to peek its rays above the tall pine trees that outlined the barn property. There was a warm humidity starting to rise, signaling a potentially warm and sticky day on the horizon. The front door of the tan metal barn was wide open allowing the fresh air breeze to filter its way down the aisle. The horses were all munching peacefully on their breakfast while last-minute checks were taking place before the big trip.

"Everything's loaded up then?" the somewhat unfriendly but experienced truck driver asked me. He looked gruff on the outside, graying beard and typical trucker hat with buttoned down plaid shirt. Deep inside I could tell he had a kind heart toward animals. At least that was what I was hoping for.

I had spent the last three weeks packing and repacking for this trip so no, I wasn't sure if everything was loaded up or not. I had the saddle, bridles, girths, saddle pads, and all the colorful polo wraps I could find packed into the tack stall in the shipping trailer. This was the first time in my entire life that I wasn't the one hauling my own horse. I was extremely nervous yet extremely thankful to not have the burden of traveling alone.

I had hired someone, someone with border crossing experience, to haul my young Hanoverian gelding across the Canadian border. It was a trip I had been dying to take for several years, but until recently had little to no funding to do. After saving up for the past three years my dream was finally coming true, and I was nervous as all get out. I would be spending the next three months with Olympic trainer Amy Arnot as a working student. The majority of my tasks would include barn chores, but I would also be receiving lessons from Ms. Arnot on Indie and hopefully on some of her schoolmasters as well.

"Yes, I think," I replied. Indie, my not-so-patient horse, was the last big item to pack, so to speak, so I quickly walked down to his stall and led him to his awaiting chariot. Indie, a big fan of traveling, was more than willing to hop in and experience a new adventure.

We stepped onto the gravel drive and only took one hesitant step toward the trailer, a chance to take a second to look at the huge rig he was about to enter. Apparently, it met Indie's approval and with one delicate step he lifted himself into the trailer.

The doors locked behind us and I was alone for about thirty seconds to say a quick prayer over my horse, the love of my life, and wipe away the tears before I stepped out the man door on the side of the trailer. Indie was certainly traveling in style. He had his own box stall with sawdust and would only be traveling with one other horse. That made me happy because Indie was quite the social butterfly, and I knew he would enjoy the company during the eight-hour "flight" to upper Ontario. They would be making two stops along the way. One in northern New York to pick up another horse, and another stop just over the Canadian border for checks.

"We'll see you there," the driver said as he gave me a quick but firm handshake. He strode away to the cab of the truck and pulled himself in, filling out a bit of paperwork before starting the engine. It was all I could do not to start crying again. What was my problem? It's not like I would never see the big brown horse ever again. I guess it was just separation anxiety kicking in. My mom put her arm around me and offered her reassurance.

"He hasn't left the driveway yet. You could always run after him and say you've changed your mind," she said. Wishful thinking on her part. She didn't want me to go but was supportive of my decision anyway. I could see the tears just ready to start pouring out from behind her glasses. This trip was going to be difficult for her as well. She was the ultimate horse show mom and had always traveled with me and my sister to shows, clinics, and everywhere else we went with the horses. I wanted to pack her up in my suitcase and take her with me, but I knew I had to do this alone.

"Thanks, mom, but we're doing this. Besides, I'll only be gone three months. I do have a job to get back to, hopefully." I am a first-grade teacher and had to take some leave of absence here at the end of the school year to actually get my three months in before school started again. My mom was willing to tear down and set up my room for me while I was gone so I could live my dream, which she hoped would be short-lived.

"Alright," I said with an anxious sigh. "Let's double check the car to make sure I've got all my stuff. I don't want to have to buy anything while I'm up there." We walked over to my little blue car and made sure all my pink suitcases were packed in and accounted for. My sister had strategically packed the Tetris of suitcases which I knew I would never in a million years be able to duplicate for the trip home, but that wasn't really a worry of mine at the moment.

My sister handed me a small package as I closed the trunk.

"Here," she said. "It's to help remind you of where you came from and hopefully encourage you to do so much more."

I opened the wrapping and found a handmade journal. Each

page had a picture of Indie, from his baby years on the farm to his present stunning condition. On the opposite pages were blank lines where I would record everything that I learned, experienced, cried about, and rejoiced about during my trip. My eyes decided to rebel and the flood gates opened. I grabbed my sister in a huge hug and together we cried tears of joy mixed with tears of sadness.

We broke our embrace moments later when I decided I needed to compose myself for my long journey. I didn't want puffy eyes for my arrival at a professional training facility.

I chose to leave my cell phone at home and instead just use the local barn phone to make the necessary calls home to let everyone know I was doing okay. I figured the international charges would become outrageous with all the talking and texting I would want to do from the barn. Besides, I was at the point in my life where pretty much all of my friends had gotten married, moved away, and started families so I really had no attachments to the area. There was no boyfriend that I needed to keep in contact with and my barn friends would stay connected with me through my family. Our barn was just a small family-run barn with only a few boarders who were more like friends than business transactions. Most of our boarders had been with us for twenty years or so.

Yes, we are certainly blessed with some wonderful horse people in our lives.

Together, my mom, my sister, and I walked up to my house one last time to make sure I had not forgotten a thing. I was certain something of great importance might have fallen behind the bed or slipped under the couch, but I did not find anything that would have been of use to me on my trip.

My sister had packed a giant bag of snacks for me to munch on during the car ride. She made sure there was nothing that would be of question when I came to the border. Although I would be stopping several times to use the restroom due to my cashew-sized bladder, I would not take the time to stop for "real" food. Just a quirk of mine. My patience with people was nowhere near my patience with my horses. Maybe that was why my best friends were four-legged kinds as opposed to the two-legged counterparts.

After a quick early lunch with my parents I said my final goodbyes back in the barn parking lot. I had to keep reminding myself that I would see them again soon. It didn't really help but at least it was a distraction. I tucked myself into my well-cared-for and well-packed car.

"There's no hurry to Canada so take your time on the roads. If there is bad weather pull over and if you get tired pull over and rest," my mom jabbered on.

"Mom, I'll be fine. Just keep praying for safe travels and all will be fine. Trust me. And don't worry. If any of those things should come up I'll remember to follow your advice." I smiled reassuringly to my mom as the tears started to well up in her eyes.

"Stop, your going to make me cry!" I jumped out of the car and gave her one last big hug. I gave my dad and sister one last hug as well hoping that I could pull this off and make everyone proud of me. As weird as it sounds, I took one last good whiff of the country air and settled back into the car, rolling the window down so I could wave my goodbyes down the driveway.

I waved the entire way as I pulled out of the driveway and said a quick prayer for myself as I headed north to the highway.

"Lord, give me strength. Give my family strength. Let your angels watch over this car and Indie's trailer and let us be a light to everyone we encounter on this awesome adventure you've allowed us to experience. You are so good!"

With that I felt energized and cranked up my Jamie Grace CD as I turned on Judy, my portable GPS system. Yes, everyone names their GPS. Don't act so surprised.

****

My trip was going quite well. My energy drink was halfway gone. One box of Raisinets were already emptied and I had just opened the trail mix when I decided it was time for my first stop. Thankfully, the traffic was very light for a sunny Monday afternoon. We had been having wonderful weather in the upper 70s and I was hoping that the farther north I would go the cooler it would get. I'm a cool-weather rider. My horse throws off some massive body heat when I ride him and I always tell people it's like riding a sauna. I wear short-sleeve shirts in the 20-degree Ohio winters because Indie is my personal heater. People think I'm crazy but until you climb aboard the steam engine you really have no idea.

After settling back into the car I turned Judy back on and headed toward the highway again. I kept thinking that if my sister were with me she would be snapping pictures with her phone at each state crossing and at all the weird sights during the trip. I was really missing her and the fact that I had no phone to call her to tell her everything I was seeing. Not that the vineyards were all that terribly exciting but to hear her voice would be good enough for me.

Before crossing into Canada I made one last stop and took some pictures with my camera before waiting in line to show my passport and answer all those scary questions about the reason for my travels. Border crossings can be quite intimidating.

I was right about the long lines. It was pretty lengthy but it moved along quickly. When I pulled up to the booth the highly unfriendly attendant took my passport and asked me exactly what I expected.

"What is your purpose for traveling to Canada?" he asked.

Oh my gosh. I knew this question was coming but I started to panic thinking I couldn't say I was traveling with my horse to ride. I wasn't technically traveling with my horse. He was staring impatiently at me and I realized it was time to suck it up and give him an answer.

"I'm visiting a farm in upper Ontario."

"Who is traveling with you?"

Okay, seriously? I'm literally the only person in the car, clearly, and you are asking me if there is anyone else traveling in my car? Yes, you got me. I have them stuffed in the trunk. But I held back the sarcasm and answered politely, "No, just me."

"How long do you plan on staying?"

"Three months."

He handed me my passport and motioned me forward into the foreign country. I was thrilled but then realized I had no idea where I was going. Apparently Judy and I were not on speaking terms at that moment either. I kindly reminded her that just because we crossed a border it doesn't mean her job was over. They still speak English up here you know. Thankfully I had a hard copy of the directions and was able to easily maneuver onto the right highway.

I kept wondering how Indie was doing. My mom's phone number was listed as the emergency number just in case something were to happen. Oh, I didn't want to even let my mind go there. I needed a distraction.

I had planned some extra time to stop at Niagara Falls for

about an hour before continuing my trek up north. It took a few swipes past the falls before finding a free parking lot (which was very difficult to do at the tourist trap, I mean natural wonder). The mist was unbelievable and breathtaking and for a moment I had forgotten that I wasn't there on vacation. After securing my car I grabbed the camera and walked to the falls, following the throngs of people to find the best viewing spot.

It actually felt good to get out and stretch my legs a bit so I didn't mind the long walk. I snapped a bunch of pictures and was totally taken in by the awesome power of the falls. It had been years since I was there and I suddenly realized that you can't fully understand God's awesome power when you're that little, but come your late twenties you start to see all the ways your life is so meaningful in His eyes.

After about twenty pictures of the falls I went into Tablerock and looked for some souvenirs. I suffered through the crowds because I knew I wouldn't be back for quite some time. I wasn't planning on buying much but then I saw the cutest t-shirt. It was white with little rhinestone eyes and a rhinestone nose with a caption underneath that said: "Canadian Polar Bear in a snow storm." How perfect for my sister! Our college mascot was the polar bear and she had been collecting odd polar bear things ever since. I just had to get her one.

Flipping through the rack I finally found her size and started heading over to the checkout counter.

"Excuse me?" I heard someone say. At first I ignored the male voice since I certainly didn't look like a local or a salesperson for that fact.

"Excuse me?" I heard him say again. I turned to see a man standing by the same t-shirts I had just come from. Without moving my head I shifted my eyes from side to side realizing there really was no one else in the area except for me. I looked at him and replied, "um, yes?" Really, what else was there to say.

"I feel really silly," he started. Good English. Must be American. Was that a racist thought? Nah. I've heard some stuff about Canadians and how they feel about us so I don't actually feel that bad about my thought process. I took a few steps in his direction.

"My sister loves polar bears and I don't know her size but she looks about your height. Can I ask what size I should get?" Not wanting to get any more information about him or his sister I quickly flipped through the shirts and handed him one that looked like it would fit me.

"This should do it. I guess it must be a sister thing," I smiled. There I go. Oversharing again. I told myself that was one thing I was really going to try to control during this trip. One of my many downfalls. It's like an open invitation to start an unwanted conversation with me. Here it comes.

"So your sister is a polar bear fanatic as well, eh?" And there it was. I might have misjudged the whole he-must-be-American comment. The "eh" was a dead giveaway.

"Yes," good job keeping the answer simple I thought. I turned and swiftly walked to the checkout counter only to realize it was the only checkout counter and my new-found friend was joining me in line. Keep your eyes forward and look annoyed I told myself. People don't bother you when you look ticked. I learned that from my friend Kathryn.

I was thankful to make my purchase and started to walk toward the door. I threw a quick last-minute glance and smile to the polar bear man, and oh my, he was quite handsome. Why hadn't I noticed before? Maybe I shouldn't have been so cold. Perhaps I should have been a little kinder to this handsome stranger. So much for shining my light. Next time, I guess.

Back in the car I had that urge to call my sister and tell her what I found for her. I didn't know if I could wait three months to give it to her. Suddenly sadness washed over me. Again, the prayer slipped from my lips, "Lord give me strength." I could do this and I would try harder to shine that silly light of mine that apparently hadn't been used in a while. I almost forgot how it worked.

Chapter Two

A few hours after I left the falls I pulled up to a gorgeous, large, black wrought iron gate that led me to a perfectly manicured gravel driveway surrounded by tall trees that were just starting to bud. The sun was still shining as I pulled up to the barn. The main barn was painted a dark gray with white trim and had a matching attached indoor arena right behind it with an Olympic-sized outdoor dressage ring right off the left side of the arena.

The white wooden fences looked recently painted and encompassed the entire barn property. That was a comforting feeling. No one wants their horse to get loose at home let alone in a foreign country where you don't know the surrounding territory. Those fences might come in handy if Indie decides to get loose.

There were two main doors into the horse barn, each with beautiful window grilles and matching hayloft windows right above the doors. Flower baskets hanging from either side of the barn looked impeccably cared for and I had to stop myself from thinking: who takes care of all this stuff? I knew the American answer but I didn't know how the Canadians pulled it off.

There were no signs of weeds in the gravel driveway, unlike at home where the weeds grow faster in the driveway than in the pasture. I was happy to see the nearby woods surrounding the dressage ring because they reminded me of home. I think it will also help Indie settle into a new atmosphere as well. Again, my thoughts drifted to my poor horse trapped in that trailer for all that time with a stranger ….

No, I knew he was fine. He had more room in his box stall than I had in my car.

I parked my car next to a Lexus sports car and started to wonder if I was in over my head working with such upper-class people. What if I don't fit in because I can't afford to fit in with these people? I'm not even sure who I will be working with during the next three months. All I know is that there will be a total of three working students, all of us from the United States.

I mustered up as much confidence as I could and walked boldly into the barn. I instantly recognized the lead trainer, Amy Arnot, two-time U.S. Olympic rider and World Equestrian Games silver medalist at the last games. I tried to contain myself from running up to her and shaking her hand like some crazed fan, begging her for an autograph and thinking I'd never wash that hand again. Foolish thoughts. I was about to spend the next ninety days with this woman. Plenty of time for autographs later.

I had heard some tough stories about Ms. Arnot. She was a hard worker and I respected that in a rider. But no one likes to be yelled at or feel like the scum on the bottom of someone else's riding boot. I was hoping that I would form my own opinion and gently reminded myself of that light I was supposed to be shinning.

"Hi, Ms. Arnot. I'm Dana Berrelli, your working student from Ohio," I said as I approached with an outstretched hand. She reached out with a smile. Good start.

"Glad you made it and welcome to AAA Equestrian Centre. Hope you had good travels." Wow. What a fantastic German accent she has! I hope I will be able to understand her when she is barking commands at me later.

"Let me show you where you will stay and then you can get settled in before we get to work." No rest for the weary here.

Ms. Arnot led me down the barn aisle, which was perfectly swept, past a row of freshly cleaned stalls on my right, to a simple white door that said "Welcome" in wooden letters. Inside, the room was neatly arranged with two twin beds, a small kitchen table, a few cabinets, a microwave, and a fridge. It was small but enough room for all I was going to be using it for over the next few months.

"This room you will share with Gertrude, a fellow rider from New Hampshire. The washroom is the next door over and there is a washer and dryer down the other barn aisle should you need to do any laundry." I had hoped to bring plenty of underwear but ninety pairs did seem a bit extreme. Yes, I would need to use the laundry room.

I followed her out of the "Welcome" room and to the next door over labeled "Washroom" where I found our bathroom facilities. Okay, it's a bit odd that I have to walk six feet down the barn aisle when I have to use the bathroom in the middle of the night, but I did happen to pack a flashlight. Thanks mom for reminding me. You never know when you're going to be left in the dark.

The bathroom was nice and simple. Sink, toilet, and shower. All I need after a long day of riding and sweating. I will become best friends with this room. It was almost nicer than my bathroom at home. The tiles were spotless and it smelled of fresh flowers. I was trying not to be jealous.

"Everyone is responsible for cleaning the bathroom. I leave that up to you girls to decide on a cleaning schedule. Same goes for the bedroom and eating area," she spoke as she continued down the aisle toward the arena. I kept my thoughts to myself hoping that my fellow riding mates would be just as clean and neat as I was.

We walked to her 70 x 200-foot indoor arena complete with viewing area, overhead watering system, three mirrored walls, and what looked like the perfect footing. There were gigantic fans attached to the ceiling and large doors on all three sides of the arena. A sound system was quietly playing some type of Mozart-like music above our heads which made the enormousness of the arena seem more tranquil and not quite as intimidating.

I flashed back to our arena back home where Indie and I always rode to music, slightly more upbeat and contemporary, but music nonetheless. Ms. Arnot caught my attention as she continued walking to the viewing area.

"This area is heated in the winter and air conditioned in the summer. You probably won't be spending much time in here due to our busy schedule but it is available to you should the opportunity present itself."

There it was. I started to feel like I had just transformed from student to slave. Oh well. Hopefully I will have some opportunities to use this wonderful place of rest. There was a couch with a table full of horse related magazines, a fridge, a coffee pot, and a wall laden with posters from various equestrian competitions. I glanced out the viewing window and took a few moments to watch the ride taking place. I followed Ms. Arnot back out into the arena where we continued to watch for a few moments.

There was a girl riding a medium-sized, probably 16 hand, gray warmblood, which I recognized as Rinaldi, Amy Arnot's silver medal winning stallion. I stood watching with great respect at the amazing suspension the horse possessed as he passaged around the short side of the arena. The girl acknowledged Ms. Arnot with a nod and continued riding forward to the most beautiful extended trot across the diagonal. I most definitely might be out of my league here, but I had complete confidence that Indie could be just as grand as Rinaldi. I just hoped I could keep up with him when he did learn those brilliant movements.

"Good, Anabella. Keep him more soft in the bridle during that extension. He tends to hang on the bit too much when he gets excited." Anabella nodded and continued riding. I made a mental note about Anabella: she nods a lot.

"The riding schedule is posted daily on the board by the door here," she pointed at a white board with several horse names listed, "so please check to see which horses are needed and when it is your time for your private lesson with your own horse. We have many horses here that need to get worked so we must follow the time schedule precisely to ensure all the horses get their proper training time. I have a list of the horses you will be responsible for tacking up and riding. Follow me."

And off she went through the arena and down the adjacent barn aisle. It looked identical to my aisle of residence with the exception of a third white door with the label "Office" in wooden letters. Another mental note: this woman really likes labels.

Her office was decent size with a wooden desk, a laptop, a filing cabinet, and tons of pictures and ribbons of not only her but other riders as well. There was a simple wallpaper border running along the top of the wall with black and yellow checkers. The walls were painted the same yellow which reminded me of the German Hanoverian colors. I took a closer look at the different riders in the professional photographs and realized it was nice to know that she shares the spotlight. She must have noticed my wandering eye.

"These are all students of mine who have competed successfully at FEI." Her tone was proud, even if a bit cocky but hey, who am I to complain if her students are doing well? That was why I was there as well.

"I have your resume here," she started as she sat behind the wooden desk. "It says your horse was the Training Level Champion for Region 2 as a three-year-old. He is also currently schooling Prix St. George as a nine-year-old. Did you do anything in between his three-year-old and nine-year-old year?"

Ouch. Her tone was totally German and I suddenly felt like an ant scampering around for a way out of the question. What was I doing here? Why did I think wasting this woman's time was to my benefit? I felt my brain ready to start oversharing again.

"Um, he's had some injuries that made him take several months off in a row on more than one occasion. He's been fine since then but I decided that going to regionals wasn't going to be worth the financial offsetting until we were able to compete at the FEI level to make it worth my time and his effort. I feel Indie, that's his barn name, I feel that he has so much more potential than I am able to bring out in him alone and I think this experience would certainly do us both good."

I paused to take a breath and to try to remember what I had just spewed out of my mouth. Ms. Arnot looked at me as if to say 'stop talking' so I did.

"I didn't see a reference to a regular trainer or lesson schedule. Who is your trainer?" she inquired.

Um, God is my trainer. But I knew she might view that as sarcasm and I've been really trying to keep that to a minimum, at least out loud.

"My trainer lives in Maryland and I only get to see him about two to three times a year." I left it at that and she seemed to be rather amused by my comment. I could almost feel her thinking 'why am I wasting my time on this nobody?'

That was the truth, though. My sister and I did all the training ourselves and relied on Rob, our Maryland trainer, to give us tips on exercises to do to help us continue up the levels when we did get the chance to ride with him.

After a moment's pause she continued.

"Alright then. Here are the horses you will be responsible for taking care of," she started, handing me a piece of paper with a relatively long list of horses. It included all their feeding and turnout instructions as well as the phone numbers of Anabella and the veterinarian.

"I expect them to be groomed, tacked, and cooled properly. If you have any questions you can ask Anabella. She is my lead instructor when I am out of town. She has been here for five years and knows all the horses and will able to tell you what you need to know. I have also hired a new manager who will be starting this week as well. You are expected to cooperate with all my employees as well as the other working students. I will be available as well. You can get in touch with me through Anabella. Any questions?"

Of course, but what actually came out was, "No, ma'am. I look forward to seeing what you can do with me." I smiled at her and took one last glance at the wall because I had a feeling I would probably never see the inside of that glorious shrine again. I want to be up on that wall, too. She must have been reading my thoughts because she stood from her desk and walked over to me.

"Work hard, train right, and devote yourself to the sport and maybe someday you'll be up there as well." Her firm voice was broken by a subtle smile and I knew right then that she liked me. At least I hoped she did.

Chapter Three

After a brief tour of the large tack room with individual wooden tack boxes, the enclosed grain and the hay room, and Indie's new home, I decided it would be best to start unpacking my car and bringing my suitcases to the "Welcome" door. I'm not quite sure what to call it. My bedroom? My kitchen? My living space?

During my thought process I heard gravel crunching under tires and started getting excited thinking Indie had arrived. I turned to look down the long aisle but to my disappointment only saw a bright red sports car pulling in the drive. Really? What do people do up here for a living to own such nice cars? I dropped off my first round of suitcases into the room and started back down the aisle to grab another load of stuff from the trunk.

A young girl stepped out of the red sports car after she had parked right next to mine. Great. I feared this snob was my "Welcome" roommate. Time to shine.

"Hello," I said as I got closer to her.

"Hello," was her short reply. But I don't think that was snob I saw. I think it was more like terror hidden behind her dark complexion. Her long black hair looked as if she had just stepped out of a beauty salon on her way to prom. She looked about that young as well. She had on designer jeans, boots that I wouldn't in a million years dream of wearing in a barn, and a navy blue designer polo shirt.

"I'm Dana, one of Ms. Arnot's working students." Good start I thought to myself.

"Oh, good," she said with what sounded like relief. "I'm Gertrude. I'll be staying as a working student as well. Am I late?" The poor girl looked simply terrified.

"Your timing is perfect. Follow me. I'll take you inside where Ms. Arnot is working. So you're from New Hampshire?" I asked, trying to ease her tension.

"Yes, it was quite the drive. I got a late start because my boyfriend got stuck in traffic on his way over to my house to say goodbye," she said, relaxing a bit as we walked. Oh good. Another oversharer. We were going to get along great. Our age gap was probably almost ten years but I'm used to working with kids so I was prepared for just about anything.

"Plus," she continued, "I had to stop along the way. There is a huge mall about three hours from my home and I figured now would be the best time to take advantage of a good shopping spree. I had to rearrange everything in my trunk after all the stuff I bought," she said, barely taking a breath.

Great. I hope she doesn't talk this much on a regular basis.

Together we walked down the aisle adjacent to our room. The smell of horses was such a comfort that I tuned Gertrude out for a moment. I wonder how everything back at our barn is going? Did the horses miss Indie? I knew they could manage without me but I still felt like I was missing out on doing my share of the responsibilities.

I dropped Gertrude off in the office with Ms. Arnot and continued to unpack my bags. It was peaceful to know I was finally here, getting settled in, but my nerves were still on edge waiting for Indie to arrive. I met up with Gertrude about thirty minutes later in our room. I helped her bring in her bags and we decided who was going to get which bed.

"So tell me a little about your horse," I started as we were re-arranging our new home.

"She's a fabulous imported Swedish warm blood. She's twelve and currently we are schooling Prix St. George. My trainer found her for me and just last year let me start riding her during lessons," Gertrude informed. Okay, so she might be a nice girl but someone in her family has way too much money.

"How long have you owned her?" I asked.

"I've owned her for three years. Before her I had a Hanoverian schoolmaster that helped me learn my tempis. I showed him fourth level for three years but he had to retire. And you?"

"I have a nine-year-old Hanoverian gelding out of Weltmeyer that I've owned since he was two and a half years old." So sue me for throwing Weltmeyer's name around. That was all I had to throw around. Weltmeyer was one of the world's leading dressage stallions standing at stud in Germany. She politely looked impressed but her self-absorption led her to continue to talk about herself. No worries. I would be spending plenty of time with her. She'd know who I was by the end of these three months.

We had just sat down at the kitchen table when we heard a knock on our door. I jumped up to answer and found Ms. Arnot standing outside the door, her breeches and boots looking spotless with every blond hair tucked neatly into a bun.

"Come, ladies. I need to introduce you to my lead instructor and manager. Plus, our final working student is here." Like obedient children we followed her down the aisle to the viewing area. Inside, there were three other people waiting for us. I didn't recognize Anabella right away. Who knew that petite girl hiding under that hard hat riding Rinaldi was actually a mid-forties trainer with long red hair? Amazing what hard hats do for people when they are aboard a horse. Mental note: quit judging people.

There was a tall, extremely slender young man standing by the window in very stylish clothing, almost too nice to wear to the barn as well. Okay, I know I said no judging but it was painfully obvious that he would not be hitting on me or Gertrude during our stay. I was actually excited when I realized he was the other working student. Indie loved men regardless of their, well, preferences.

"This is Arthur, from New York. He'll be on the schedule with you two. Please learn each other's horses and the care that they need in case we need to rotate schedules or horses." Arthur had walked over to me and Gertrude and shook both of our hands. The horses must really like his delicate grip. I need to start practicing that grip.

I got the feeling Ms. Arnot meant one of us might be acquiring more horses due to someone else's inability to care for so many animals at once. Since I was apparently the oldest I was probably the target for acquiring those extra horses. Good for me. I'll show Ms. Arnot that I'm here truly to learn and not just look pretty. With that thought I glanced down at my traveling jeans, paddock boots, and bright yellow polo shirt with the Hanoverian emblem embroidered on it. This was about as pretty as I was willing to get anyway.

"Edvard?" Ms. Arnot called out in her German accent. Edward must be the new manager she was talking about. He walked over from the coffee pot where he had been trying to brew coffee since we walked in earlier.

"This is Edvard, our new manager. He's also my nephew but that does not allow for any preferential treatment," Ms. Arnot said as she introduced Edward to the rest of us. I'm not certain but I may have audibly gasped when I saw his face. I could feel my cheeks flushing with, what was it, embarrassment perhaps? He smiled at me and walked over to shake my hand first.

"Hi, fellow polar bear lover." Wow. Who would have guessed in a million years that I would be face to face once again with the man I had met at the souvenir shop just a few hours earlier? Why did I have to realize he was so handsome back there in line? I should have just kept to myself as usual. My smile was sincere as I said a sheepish "hi" in return. He continued to shake Gertrude's hand, and then Arthur's. I could tell Arthur was having the same feelings I was having.

My thought process started going haywire as I secretly hoped Edward might have more interest in Arthur than myself or Gertrude. That would certainly make working with him easier.

Edward looked absolutely amazing in a hunter green embroidered polo shirt. His gray-blue eyes were mesmerizing and I suddenly realized that I might have just missed some conversation. I quickly snapped back to reality as Ms. Arnot broke my concentration.

"I just received a call from the driver of Arthur's and Dana's horses. He'll be here in an hour. Please go prepare your stalls," Ms. Arnot stated as she closed her cell phone. I temporarily forgot about Edward as the announcement of Indie's arrival made me jump with joy, literally. I was suddenly grounded when I realized everyone was staring at me. Am I the only person who actually enjoys the simple company of my horse? I smiled as I simply stated, "Sorry, I'm just a little excited to see my boy."

Gertrude followed me out of the viewing room and over to Indie's stall. She had started some mindless chatter as I emptied the three bags of shavings in the stall, smoothing them out to make for an inviting welcome. I filled up two water buckets and threw in a flake of hay since I knew he would be hungry. He's always hungry.

Feeding was one of the many downfalls of a 17.2 hand, ADD-prone work machine. I'm talking about Indie of course. It took me a while to find the right mix of feed that wouldn't make him more hyper but would still stick to his ribs. I checked the feed stores in the area before I had left home and found one nearby that sold the same pelleted hay and 14 percent feed that I use at home. I loaded a bag of each from home into the trailer before Indie left just in case something was different. I had also packed a ninety-day supply of his supplement in the trailer.

At some point Gertrude had left and started working on her own stall. Although the constant chatter might get to me every now and then I knew we would get along well enough.

Anxious and not knowing what to do with myself while I waited, I walked through the two barns memorizing all the horses, and not just the ones I was responsible for during my stay. I saw Gertrude had gone back to our room to make a phone call, probably to the boyfriend. I figured I would make my call home after Indie had arrived and had settled in to his 12 x 12 stall.

I found Anabella preparing another horse to ride so I walked over and decided to get some information about the muscular, chestnut horse she was tacking.

"This is Madrid, my fifteen-year-old Quarter Horse," she spoke softly but with authority. I tried not to show the shock on my face but I think she saw it regardless.

"He's beautiful," I replied. Back home, we have the AQHA, American Quarter Horse Association. If a Quarter Horse is born in Canada is there such a thing as the CQHA? Should I look stupid and ask? Maybe I'll just have to look it up later.

"He belonged to my husband but I just couldn't seem to part with him after my husband passed away. He's such a good horse, even temperament, gentle spirit, well-balanced. I've shown him lower level dressage but his joy is just being here at the barn with his friends." Her simple nod told me the conversation was over. So I moved on.

After one more swipe through the barn I went to the viewing area, taking advantage of probably my only opportunity to use it during my stay. I really had no responsibilities until Indie arrived so I tried to soak up as much atmosphere as I could. Checking my watch I realized I had about twenty minutes before the trailer arrived. I tried to sit on the well-worn maroon and blue plaid couch but ended up pacing the viewing windows instead, watching Anabella and her mighty steed grace the arena.

"Hey, Polar Bear," I heard as the door shut behind him. Startled, I jumped and grabbed my chest as if implying I was having a heart attack.

Although his tone seemed friendly there was an underlying superiority edge in Edward's voice. Great. He's one of those men who thinks they have all the power and can boss you around just because they can. I guess that is typically what managers do but whatever. I'm not liking this awkward connection we have.

"Oh, hi. I didn't hear you come in," I said, cool, calm and finally collected. "I apologize but I didn't catch your name earlier, Mr. ...." I thought it best to try to establish a professional relationship with my new manager.

"Please, call me Edward. Mr. Olsen sounds too much like I should be on *Little House on the Prairie*," he said casually as he walked over to the refrigerator. I was still somewhat put off by this man, but his calm and casual demeanor showed that he had no clue. So he watched, or at least knew of, *Little House on the Prairie*. Perhaps he was closer to my age than I originally had him pegged. His neatly trimmed and slightly spiked dirty blond hair and clean shaven face made him appear much younger.

"Or I could just call you Willie and make it that much easier to remember," I said aloud, chuckling to myself. To my surprise he chuckled as well. Wow, someone who got my bizarre sense of humor. That just might make these next few months a little easier.

"The funny part is my sister, the polar bear lover, is named Eleanor, or Nellie for short. Rough life for her trying to always prove she wasn't the stuck up snob that her namesake portrayed on TV."

I smiled, reminiscing about old childhood memories of the show. For a moment I actually started feeling comfortable around Edward. He had a very warm smile that could easily be mistaken for someone who was just trying to put on the charm. I wasn't completely sure about him yet. Was he sincere or was he just good at his job?

"Dana!" Gertrude called as she burst through the viewing room doors. "Your boy is here!" I practically ran to the door before remembering I was in the middle of a conversation. I turned to Edward and apologized, again.

"So sorry. It was nice talking with you Willie," I said, trying to keep the mood light and hoping I wasn't being offensive or unprofessional. I guess it was a little too late for that now.

"No worries, Polar Bear. Go take care of your horse," he smiled. Oh, what a smile. I could just look at that straight row of teeth all day, but perhaps some other day. Right now my horse was here and I was starting to realize how uncomfortable Indie must feel from being stuck in a trailer for so long.

Arthur caught up with me and Gertrude on the way out to the parking lot. I hadn't realized how tall he was until he was standing next to my average 5'6" frame. He had to be at least 6'3" or so it seemed. I was really curious to see his mammoth beast come off the trailer.

"Oh, I hope Donny didn't cause too much trouble on the way up here," Arthur said in a small voice that did not match his body structure. I suppressed a laugh and then worried, if his horse isn't a good traveler, how did that affect Indie? I quickly sped up my pace and beat Arty (he deserves that nickname) to the trailer.

"Both horses did just fine. I do have to say, I think yours is about ready to bounce out of his box though," the truck driver said, pointing to me.

Oh great. I guess I'm stuck with psycho pony for the next few hours until he burns off some of his energy.

Arthur's horse came off the trailer first. He was an elegant type warmblood, very fine boned, approximately 16.3 hands, with a very light step. His light bay coat was shiny and clean and he looked positively as proud as his owner. I admit he was quite impressive.

By that time Ms. Arnot had joined the three of us riders out in the parking lot. I quickly walked into the trailer and politely asked if I could unload my horse myself. Perhaps he would not make such a bad first impression that way. Indie has a tendency to give people the wrong idea of the type of horse he truly is. His eyes might say he is sweet and innocent but his brain is that of an extremely curious two-year-old.

"He's all yours," the driver said as he handed me the lead line. I stepped up into the trailer and slid the chain over his nose. In my experience that was the only way I could let Indie know that I was in charge, not him. He has a tendency to forget, frequently.

I don't know if it was the Canadian air or that fact that Indie saw all the expensive cars in the parking lot but he walked off the trailer as if he was King Henry himself. His head was held high, his steps were light but definite, and his muscles rippled like that of a world-class athlete. I was proud and scared all at the same time. Who was this horse and what did he do to Indie?

As I walked him past Ms. Arnot I could see her checking him out. Was she secretly criticizing him or was she thinking that I'm in over my head with too much horse? Indie was a whopping 17.2 hands high and only looked bigger because of his long but well-defined neck. I led Indie into the barn and right to his stall. If there is one thing I know about my horse it is the fact that the first thing he always does when he gets to a show is pee in his freshly laid bedding.

I led him in his stall and quickly locked the door once I had let myself out. He circled twice like a dog before letting loose.

"Such a good boy," I praised. It was not that uncommon to randomly praise your horse for doing something God intended them to do in the first place. It made up for all the times you corrected them for doing those things unintended, like bucking you off or bolting as fast as they could all the way across the ring.

"You certainly have a handsome horse there," Edward said as he approached the bars of the stall. His eyes didn't leave Indie as he spoke, nor did mine.

"You certainly aren't going to be making this escapade easy for yourself coming in here with a horse like that," he continued with no humor found in his voice. I shot a glance over at him and suddenly realized he was only standing about two feet away from me. His voice was quiet as he spoke, as if he didn't want anyone else to hear.

"What do you mean?" I asked just as quiet, but all I got was a pair of stern, brilliant gray eyes staring at me. Everything in me shook and I didn't know what to do. My mind was searching for something to say but I couldn't think. Indie literally just got there and now the mood had suddenly changed at the barn. Was it Edward's captivating eyes staring so intently at my soul or was it that threat that worried me? Edward walked away and threw me one last piece of advice before taking his eyes off me.

"You best be careful. And watch your back."

Chapter Four

Gertrude's horse arrived about an hour after Donny and Indie. Jasmine was just as beautiful as Gertrude had described. She was black with four white socks which I envied terribly. Indie has no white on his dark brown body except for a very small white spot on his forehead called a star. I'd die for a horse that had so much chrome and I'm certain Gertrude's family paid a pretty penny for Jasmine.

I followed Gertrude and Jasmine to their stall and commented on how beautiful her horse was. I also helped her take off the horse's leg wraps and added some hay to her stall. Simple stuff really, but apparently Gertrude must not be used to doing all this by herself.

I tried to shake off the unsettling comment by Edward and started focusing on the task ahead. It was feeding time and we all helped each other, just so that we were all on the same page as to our daily routines. After we were finished feeding I turned my selected horses out in the pasture while Arty started tacking up Rinaldi.

Ms. Arnot was going to give us a riding demonstration as an introduction to her teaching style. I already had a good understanding of her philosophy because I did my homework before I came. I watched several of her championship rides and read up on all the magazine articles that I could get my hands on.

Instead of sitting in the viewing room the three of us chose to stand in the arena to get the full affect and to hear her comments.

Anabella had joined us halfway through the ride. She commentated on Rinaldi as Ms. Arnot put him through all the phases of the PSG test, the one we were all there to school and master. She explained fluently about every step the horse took and the aids that were necessary to complete such a task. You could tell how much passion Anabella had for her employer and for the discipline.

So far I hadn't noticed any odd behavior from the staff or the other riders so I started easing my own tension that had spiked earlier that evening with Edward. I noticed he was not around and was thankful that he was just the manager, not one of the riders that I would be working with daily. At least I hoped I would not be working with him. Watching those strong biceps pick up hay ... snap out of it, Dana!

I glanced over at Gertrude and had to do a double take. Is she seriously texting on her phone right now? What is it with this younger generation and the fact that they can not seem to be apart from their electronic appendages? At least she was trying to be discrete about it, although I told myself to remind her later that night in our room that she might want to leave that thing behind when we were working. I just shook my head and went back to watching the ride.

After we had our demonstration it was time to get out our kids and stretch their legs. We were not going to have any lessons, just an informal meet and greet for Ms. Arnot and our horses.

I was excited and nervous to bring Indie out into public. He was a good boy when he wanted to be, and quite naughty all the other times. Hopefully he would not pull the short straw that day.

I decided just getting on and riding was the best option for Indie. Lunging was not our strong suit and usually resulted with me being dragged halfway across the arena floor. Oh, yeah. It's happened, several times. If only I had a video camera I would probably be $10,000 richer. Everyone loves a good laugh, especially at someone else's expense.

Thanks to my fashionable sister she helped me pack coordinating riding outfits that would match Indie's polo wraps and saddle pad every ride. I grabbed a pair of black breeches and my Hanoverian socks, but left on my yellow polo shirt (since that was the plan anyway) and threw my do-rag on over my hair. I love having short hair but believe me, no one wants to see it after it's been under a riding helmet. It's always plastered with sweat in some unusual direction.

Gertrude was grooming up Jasmine as I walked down the aisle. Her perfect horse apparently only needed to be lunged because that was all she planned on doing with her mare that night. Arthur was on the other side of the barn so I wasn't sure what his plan was for our intro ride with Ms. Arnot. He always walked around as if everything he was doing was of major importance. Good for him.

I took my time grooming and tacking Indie because I really didn't want a lot of people around when I was riding. One could never be too sure what kind of mood Indie would be in, and if it was going to be a rodeo ride I didn't need everyone knowing right off the bat how crazy my horse could be. Gertrude was just finishing with the arena as I was entering. She was a polite young girl but not always filled with common sense. She clearly saw me walking in, even stopping to say "hi" as she turned off the arena lights.

Really? Did you think I would enjoy riding in the dark? I

guess that was one way for people to literally not see my ride. I took a moment to contemplate the idea and then thought the better choice would be to see where I was going in the arena. I waited until Gertrude walked down the aisle before I turned the lights back on.

I was searching for the switch to the music when I saw Arthur and his horse appear in the arena. There were a total of six switches on the wall. I knew the three of them that controlled the arena lights and I knew there was one for the sprinkler system and one for the music but I didn't know what the sixth one was for. What if I flipped the wrong one and some siren went off or I blew a fuse to some main part of the barn? Worse yet, what if I accidentally turned on the sprinkler when Arthur was in the arena?

Hmm. Not a bad thought, evil as it was.

Was I not paying attention earlier when Ms. Arnot was explaining everything to me? Panic started to settle in and it felt like I was standing there for an eternity looking like a complete moron for not knowing what to do next.

"If you're looking for the music it's the one above the water switch," Arthur hollered over obviously seeing my switch dilemma. "Weren't you paying attention earlier?" I could see a hint of a smile to go along with all that attitude so I decided nothing Arthur said should offend me in any way.

Although it still probably will.

"Do you mind if I turn the music on? I always do so much better when I have the distraction," I asked trying to be polite.

"Distraction, honey? We are in a different country in a strange barn. What more of a distraction do you need? But sure, I don't mind. Donny's all about classical all the way up to his training method." So he had a point. I'm just trying to feel more at home and now Arthur's attitude was starting to annoy me.

****

It turned out to be a good ride. We just did the basics to stretch our legs. Donny and Indie ended up getting along very well and Arthur kept to himself for most of our ride. I tried to throw a couple of glances his way every now and then to check out his horse. They looked like a good match, good rhythm, decent suspension, and very steady. In my book that would qualify as a boring ride.

I noticed that Gertrude had also joined us, by way of the viewing room, again with phone in hand. That is going to be some phone bill, but when you've got the money to cover it who really cares, I guess.

Arthur had dismounted and started walking out of the arena when Edward walked in and joined us, soon followed by Gertrude.

"We have a brief meeting in the office in thirty minutes. I expect everyone to be prompt. Ms. Arnot has weekly meetings with the staff to ensure quality care and efficiency for her farm." His tone was firm but almost forced.

There was something different about him since the first time we had actually been introduced about three hours ago. He glanced up at me, our eyes meeting briefly, before turning and walking back down the aisle. To be fair, he looked at all of us as he was talking but there was just something about those eyes — good and bad. There was a harshness that had overtaken his kind masculine features. Regardless of their appearance, his eyes were highly distracting and I couldn't afford that type of diversion over the next three months. This trip was about my training. Not my personal life.

I dismounted, untacked my horse, and put everything away in my tack locker before heading over to the office. I felt a little rushed because I didn't want to be late and give Ms. Arnot a bad impression of my efficiency. I'm one of those annoying people who always arrives thirty minutes early somewhere, just to make sure I don't miss anything. That day, though, I was hitting it right on the nose.

Arthur was just heading toward me as I opened the door to the office. Being the polite person I am I let him in first and he proudly entered the room without even thinking about chivalry. I rolled my eyes but smiled anyway.

The room was full. Anabella, Gertrude, Arthur, myself, Ms. Arnot, and Edward were all present and accounted for. Gertrude and Edward were seated in the two chairs in front of Ms. Arnot's desk while Anabella propped herself up on an adjacent table. Arthur comfortably leaned against the wall while I tried to find a resting spot myself. I was starting to get really tired, just from all the excitement from the day. It was just earlier that day that I was still at home in Ohio anxiously awaiting this adventure. Now, horse tucked in for the night, bags unpacked, shower beckoning, I was ready to crash. I still had on my riding clothes and do-rag and was really starting to wish I had grabbed a ball cap.

As soon as I started heading to a spot on the floor to what felt like curling up in a ball to sleep, I saw Edward stand up from his chair and motion for me to sit. On any regular day I would be proud and say I was fine to hunker down on the floor, but that day I wanted that chair more than anything. So I took it with a nod of thanks in his direction. So chivalry wasn't quite dead yet. I scooted over to the chair and sat, feeling good to actually sit for the first time in a long time. I couldn't help but look at Edward as I sat down and, if I wasn't mistaken, I saw the kind, friendly Willie I had met earlier. What was it with these Canadians?

The meeting only lasted about twenty minutes and I was thankful when Ms. Arnot said, "See you all in the morning. I look forward to seeing you all in action." And with that we all stood to leave.

"Ms. Berrelli, may I have a word with you before you go," Ms. Arnot spoke. I hadn't even been there twenty-four hours and I suddenly felt I was on that dreaded walk to the principal's office. Not that I actually ever took that walk, but I have definitely sent some of my students down there for their misbehavior. So I could only assume this was what it would feel like.

I noticed the rest of my comrades were only thinking of themselves because none of them offered me a sympathetic look. They just headed out the door to find peace and rest while I suffered in silence. I did happen to notice Edward exiting, eyes more interested in looking down at his feet than where he was going.

I tried to replay the day as quickly as I could in my slow brain. Did I do something wrong so soon in the game? Indie hasn't been here long enough to destroy anything, yet. And he will, and I will be ready to replace anything he chooses to "play" with while we are here. Still, nothing else came to mind.

Odd. Is this little one-on-one I am about to have with Ms. Arnot going to be related to Edward's earlier warning today? In all honesty, I wasn't sure what to expect when the door closed.

I turned back to her desk but remained standing. I didn't want to give the impression that I was looking to stay much longer than necessary.

"I may have slightly misunderstood your riding abilities earlier and I would like for you to clarify them again for me." There was no trace of a smile but her words were not completely threatening either. I took a deep breath but decided I didn't have much time for thinking so I started to mouth spew, again.

"I've been riding since I was five years old. Grew up in Pony Club. Focused much of my career on hunters and eventually jumpers and eventing before becoming reconnected with dressage. It has helped me tremendously in my jumping career as well. I never liked dressage because I thought riding around from letter to letter was kind of boring, but then when I started actually getting into the discipline I realized how terribly wrong I was." Like how terribly wrong I am right now for giving my entire life story. I feel like Chunk, the little boy on Goonies who was captured by the Fratellis and forced to give his life story.

"But who have you trained under?" She broke in, annoyed and not wanting to hear the rest of my fascinating story.

"Oh, well lessons started out with a girl down the street from me. She was into the Quarter Horse circuit. From there I got instruction from Pony Club instructors, then moved on to a friend who used to board at our barn but when that didn't work out after a few years I found Ron, my Maryland trainer. Like I said earlier, I only get to see him a few times a year so we are probably more behind in our training than we should be.

"I've never sent my horse off for training. First of all, it's not in my budget and secondly, I find it extremely rewarding to learn up the levels along with my horse. I've never ridden higher than fourth level and neither has my horse. I am a proud adult amateur and will continue until I earn that USDF gold medal. I've seen too many riders jump on their horse the day of the show after it has spent months with the trainer and expect to win. That's not what I'm looking for here." Was that enough? I really had nothing else to share.

"I see. And now you are here," she said as she gestured her hands toward the ground. "Looking for what exactly then?" she questioned although it seemed like she already knew the answer.

Without thinking I answered.

"I'm looking to get up on that wall of yours, Ms. Arnot."

Chapter Five

A strange bed had never felt so good before. I woke up at six o'clock the next morning refreshed and ready to get to work. Gertrude was mumbling something, I assume her protest for the early morning hour. I grabbed my clothes and took my six-foot walk to the bathroom. It only took me a few minutes to wash up and get dressed before heading back to the room. Gertrude was still in bed so I flipped on all the lights I could find. If we were in this together then she certainly better be up when I was. No way was I about to take care of her horses as well as mine.

I poured my cereal and ate while flipping through one of the many magazines left on the table. Gertrude finally joined me and although she hadn't even made it to the bathroom yet, she looked all made up and ready for the day. Impressive.

As I ate I recalled our conversation the night before. Gertrude had asked what Ms. Arnot had wanted to speak with me about, and although it was a private conversation I shared just a tidbit of information. I told Gertrude that we spoke about goals and that I was sure she would be talking to her and Arthur as well. Satisfied with that answer she went back to sending a few more texts before going to bed.

I dreaded yet looked forward to my lesson with Ms. Arnot that afternoon. I wasn't sure what she expected from me but I was excited to see what she could get out of us. I said a quick prayer before leaving our room to give me strength and patience. I knew no miracle breakthrough was going to happen the first day but I also knew God worked in mysterious ways.

"For I know the plans I have for you …." Jeremiah 29:11 came to mind as I put on my do-rag and headed out the door for morning feeding. It is such a reassuring feeling knowing there is a God that already has your life planned and set into action. I just need to take that action and make it for Him.

I finished feeding and turned out my four horses before starting to clean my stalls. It was easy work for me, since it was what I had been doing for the past twenty-five years of my life. I was done within the hour while Gertrude was still only halfway through. Arthur was just about finished with his work as well so I decided to head to the arena for a few minutes to see who was riding. Ms. Arnot was just finishing up with Anabella who was cooling out Rinaldi. Not wanting to waste any time, I mentally made a note of what needed to be done that day. I still had horses to turn out, feedings to do, and of course my much anticipated lesson with Ms. Arnot. I had already figured out what I was going to wear to look impressive.

I went back to Indie's stall to hand walk him for a few minutes before continuing my morning work. When I put him away ten minutes later I checked my schedule to see that I was right on time for the midday feeding. I was really liking this whole schedule- following routine I had. I never was the type to follow people around, constantly asking them what they wanted me to do next. That drives me nuts. This is so much better.

****

By evening feeding I was starting to get worried. My lesson was in an hour and I started doubting my riding abilities. I know

helping Gertrude with her horses on several occasions. I was a softy when it came to a needy person. If she hadn't been trying so hard to get her work done I certainly would not have helped her out, but it turns out she was just not cut out for the physical labor.

The three of us decided we would celebrate by heading out to dinner in town that night. Although we were all beat and knew we had to get up early the next morning we made the decision to spend at least an hour away from the barn. Me being an anti-social butterfly, I was not really looking forward to spending time with my barn mates, the same people I've been spending every waking moment with for the last week, but I thought I would be a trouper and go with them.

We were all just getting ready to head out to Gertrude's car (we chose hers because it had more room and was probably the most comfortable out of all our vehicles) when Ms. Arnot asked me into her office for a few moments.

Here we go again I thought. What more could she possible want to pry out of me now? I was already getting quite the complex from all her questions and private meetings.

"I've decided to give you two of Arthur's horses to care for," she said matter of factly as I walked into her office.

What? If anything give me Gertrude's horses, not his. He was perfectly capable of completing his own work in a timely manner. What was she trying to do? The mouth spoke before the brain could think of a better alternative.

"Arthur's not the one struggling. I'd be more than happy to take on some of Gertrude's horses instead," I said, slightly more defiantly than I intended.

"Miss Berrelli, I don't think that would be in your best interest. Starting tomorrow you will be responsible for Antiqua and Whillem as well as your own crew. Please make sure you keep to the schedule. I would hate to see your lesson time shortened due to time constraints. That's all. Have a good evening." She slid a pair of reading glasses up the bridge of her nose and picked up some paperwork. Probably nothing of importance, she just wanted me out of her office without another word.

If I was a swearing person now would be the time to start letting them rip. I walked out of her office, disgusted at how blatantly obvious her favoritism for Arthur had become. What did I do to tick this woman off and how was I going to make it the next eighty-five days of being treated this way?

Absentmindedly, I felt my back pocket looking for my phone. Argh! I didn't even have that life line to call my sister and vent with her. I took a moment to stop in the bathroom to compose myself before heading back out to the car. How was I going to handle all this and still have enough time and energy to make it through my lesson? After a few deep breaths I realized that it didn't matter. I am nothing short of a determined equestrian, seeking knowledge and not approval from Ms. Arnot.

I wondered if Arthur already knew but I decided not to ask simply because I did not know how to approach him about the subject. Who's idea was it to go out tonight anyway? Maybe I should just go tell them I'm not feeling well and that I am going to stay back. I stared at my reflection in the mirror for a moment. God might not have tapped me with the beauty wand but He certainly gave me talent. And talent is what I need to focus on right now.

Suck it up, I told myself. This is not the place to start feeling pity for yourself. I'll do my job and I'll do it better than Amy could imagine. Yes, I just dropped her respectable title and called her by her first name. I knew tomorrow I would go back to referring to her as Ms. Arnot but in my irritation she was temporarily demoted. Old habits die hard and I just couldn't disrespect my host. A few minutes later I met the two at the car and we were off to a local diner Anabella had suggested we try.

A short drive down the road and we were in town, sitting at a booth waiting for our drinks to arrive. Arthur and Gertrude were sitting directly across from me, facing the main door. We had just ordered our drinks when I saw Gertrude feverishly waving, broad smile across her face accenting her dark feminine features. Who on earth does she know here in Canada? I know she is very social and friendly but none of us have left the barn property, with the exception of a short trip to the grocery store earlier in the week. Smiling at her outward show of emotion I turned to see who she was waving to. My smile quickly disappeared as a hot red flush fell across my face. I hope no one noticed.

There was Edward, standing near the front door, a shy grin on his face as he gave a brief wave back in our direction. Very manly, of course. To my relief he did not walk over to join us even though I had already conveniently slid my body to the middle of the booth as to not offer any available seating if he did want to join us. But then I noticed a dark haired woman standing next to him. He had his hand on her back as he guided her behind the hostess to their own seating area on the other side of the diner. I was thankful they weren't sitting close-by.

I was also feeling strangely disappointed. I should have known someone as handsome as he would have a girlfriend. I hadn't really thought about him much all week since we never crossed paths at the barn anymore. Once the three of us had our schedules down pat there was no real need for Edward to be supervising us every minute of the day. The simple fact was that Edward had a girlfriend.

Oh well. Chalk it up to another one lost. That seemed the

story of my life, one I was very used to by now. The only males consistent in my life were my geldings. They might be a handful at times but they have never disappointed me, unlike their human versions. This new devolvement with Edward would actually make things easier in the barn. Less tension.

I know bitter is bad. I turned my focus back to our little group and gave my food order to the waitress who had just appeared.

The three of us made small talk, well, Gertrude did most of the talking but that was okay. I learned more about her home life than I needed to know but at least it helped pass the time.

Arthur thankfully spared us some of the details of his life, the unspoken ones that could remain unspoken for all I cared. Amazing, though. Even sitting at the table with other people he still managed to sound as if he was the only person at the diner.

The food was a nice change from the stuff we'd been eating all week. Frozen dinners, cheese and crackers, sometimes just a piece of fruit were all that were keeping me alive. It wasn't bad but I hadn't really noticed until that night how hungry I actually was. We all scarfed down our food and were so full we couldn't even possibly think of dessert.

The checks were laid on the table and after all of us chipped in for the tip we headed up to the register to pay for our meals. Who should be up there but Edward and his girl, paying the cashier. I heard the girl say she had to call the sitter and would meet him outside. Sitter equaled children in my book. Does he have children, too? No, it was none of my business.

Edward finished paying his bill and turned to say good night to all of us, lingering just a little too long as if he wanted to say something but didn't. I resisted those eyes and looked down at the money in my hand, pretending I was recounting as to avoid any further eye contact. My decisions were always being challenged, but this decision should be easy for me. Leave Edward alone and focus on the new schedule of extra horses that would start tomorrow morning. Did Edward know? Was that why he was lingering?

I looked up just in time to see him walk toward the door, not even looking back. Who cares if he knows about his aunt's evil scheme to tear me down. Let the whole world know. I'm going to show everyone just how determined I really am.

This trip was about finding my strengths and learning all I could absorb in order to go far in the horse world. This trip was not about making friends. I didn't need them. I didn't want them. I needed to keep my head clear.

But Edward would not go away. I was the last person to pay my check and had to catch up with Gertrude and Arthur since they had left the diner without me. Such great friends. I'm surprised they weren't already halfway down the road before remembering they forgot me. Mean, but possibly true.

When I got outside I saw them slowly walking to the car, Gertrude chatting poor Arthur's ear off about some other casual experience she had in her short life. Her arm was loosely looped through Arthur's as if they were the bestest of friends. Good for her. At least it's not me.

"Hey," I heard in the darkness. It took me by surprise and I jumped a bit, looking to where it came from. There to my right was Edward, a bit creepy standing on the sidewalk all by himself, the shadows enhancing his already great features. He was a good six inches taller than me so he was easily recognizable, even in the dark.

"Do you always jump when people talk to you?" he asked, all the tension gone in his demeanor. He was having a Willie moment and I wanted so desperately to ask him why the split personality, but I didn't.

"Only when creepers purposely sneak up on me," I replied offering a meaningful smile. "What's up?" I asked.

"I know what Amy said to you, not only earlier in the week but tonight as well. I'm so sorry but I had nothing to do with the change," he said sincerely.

"I wasn't planning on blaming you. Besides," I continued, positivity oozing out of my pores, "extra work just means I'll keep busy. I'm not used to just four horses anyway. We have more than that at our family farm." Right away I knew that was too much and probably came across too harsh, but I was on the defensive now. Be prepared to be shocked and amazed Amy, I mean Ms. Arnot.

Chapter Six

Saturday morning did not prove to be all that satisfying in the shock and amazement category. Arthur was completely unsympathetic to the situation and although he did not rub it in my face or give me pity, he certainly went about his business as if nothing had changed.

Gertrude felt bad for me but only because I was no longer able to help her with her work in the mornings. Nice to know she even noticed. We didn't have personal lessons on the weekends, that was Ms. Arnot's time way from her barn to travel and do clinics elsewhere around the country. We were invited to go to a clinic with her the following weekend since it was close-by but the clinic that weekend was somewhere I couldn't even pronounce.

It was a for-fun day, so to speak, to take Indie out and do whatever I wanted. Our duties were done as soon as we finished up our schedule, as long as we were back in the barn by five o'clock to do evening feedings and night checks. That really didn't leave too much free time but it was nice to know Ms. Arnot wasn't around to be watching us with her freakish hawk eye.

I didn't feel the need to tell Gertrude or Arthur what I was doing. After all, when I looked out the window around lunch time I noticed Arthur's car was already gone. Must be nice having two less horses to take care of everyday.

I found Gertrude in our room when I went in to grab my

riding breeches. She was on the phone, as usual, chatting away to her boyfriend. I showed her my pants as if that were some indication to her where I was going to be if she needed me for any odd reason. And I do mean odd reason.

The other day she came to me in a panic which immediately had me thinking the worst: something happened to one of her horses, or she got hurt, or perhaps even broke a nail. No. She was panicking over the fact the arena footing had just been freshly dragged and she was afraid of making hoof prints during her ride. Oh, the drama.

Indie and I went for a leisurely ride in the outdoor dressage ring. The fresh Canadian air felt wonderful as we walked out on a loose reign after a brief workout to stretch the limbs. I was so proud of Indie and his behavior so far on this trip. It's almost as if he, too, sensed Ms. Arnot's dislike toward us during our rides with her. He seemed determine to prove he could handle the work load and was actually doing things I hadn't dreamed he and I would be doing together as a team. I suddenly realized I was having one of those proud mama moments.

During our lessons the past week, Ms. Arnot insisted on making me feel like I wasn't trying hard enough, even though I had caught a glimpse of surprise on her face every once in a while when we proved her wrong. I tried not to let the satisfaction go to my head because, although we were there on a mission to learn, I also had to remind myself I had been given this opportunity for a much higher reason. I hadn't quite figured it out but I kept a straight face, and surprisingly, my mouth shut. It definitely was a start for me.

I took the peaceful opportunity to stroll outside our fenced boundaries toward the house on the property. It was the temporary residence of Ms. Arnot while she was in training there in Canada during the summer months. Come winter she would be taking her band of horses down to Wellington, Florida. That seems the place to be when you have lots of money and nothing better to do than spend it on your horse. I would never see that day but that was fine with me. I like my small farm in Ohio. We have everything we need right on our property. We have a barn with comfy stalls, an small indoor arena for bad weather riding, a regulation size dressage ring outback, pastures, and a small event course in our back woods. Best of all, my sister and I live right on the property to keep an eye on the horses 24/7.

It might not seem ideal to most people, being burdened with tremendous responsibility, but I find such joy and pride knowing that I am blessed with such a wonderful set up, a wonderful family, and a wonderful Creator who made it all happen.

Ms. Arnot's house was small and simple from the outside. I assumed a barn manager stayed there while she was away in the winter. It was a brick ranch, beautifully landscaped with flowers and shrubs, a cobblestone walkway that attached the house to the barn, and a fancy arbor that came off the back porch.

We didn't get too close because I didn't want to seem too nosy, or leave suspicious hoof prints, so we turned back and headed toward the barn. On the way back I noticed a strange car pulling in to the farm. Only Gertrude and myself were still there and if I wasn't mistaken Gertrude would still be lost in the cellular world, clueless to the situation around her. I quickly dismounted and brought Indie back into the barn and put him in the cross ties so I could be better prepared to find out who this visitor was.

I heard one car door close, then another, and then one more. Great. I wasn't prepared to deal with more than one person in this strange new territory. What if they didn't speak English?

The tension in my shoulders dropped a bit when I noticed

Edward walking down the aisle but then quickly tensed back up when I saw him followed by a woman and a young child, probably around six or seven. You'd think being a teacher I'd be good at determining ages but I'll be honest, they just look like kids to me.

I walked back over to Indie knowing I was no longer needed on high alert. I'm sure Edward could handle the tour without my assistance. To my dismay they stopped in front of my horse, all smiles. The child looked rather harmless but I was not about to give her the benefit of the doubt. I know how quickly those little ones can turn when they are used to getting their own way. At first they appear sweet and innocent and then quickly turn without notice, demanding and whining for attention.

"Dana," Edward started. Again, I had to look away from those captivating eyes. It felt wrong enjoying them when clearly he was there with his family. "This is my sister, Eleanor and her daughter, Mable," he finished with a dashing smile. I hope the shock that registered in my head was not as evident on my face.

"Ah, is this the sister that likes polar bears by chance?" I asked, reaching out to shake her hand. Her smile lit up the barn and I could suddenly see the resemblance in her eyes. I was still cautious of the little one.

"It's nice to meet you, Dana," Eleanor replied. "And yes, that would be me. Long story short I've spent some time with the creatures and have grown a certain attachment to them."

"Eleanor majored in animal science and has been all over Canada and Alaska studying the wildlife." Edward proved to be the ever-proud brother. Eleanor just blushed.

"Can I pet the pony?" came a small voice. I looked down to see Mable still holding her mother's hand. I also noticed that hand had a ring on her finger so I assumed there was a daddy somewhere in the picture. Bravo for the family values that so few people still shared. But my moment's hesitation had opened the door for Edward to cut in and save the day.

"Indie is a little tired from his workout. Why don't we find a horse that is ready to be petted?" Well if that doesn't beat all. Totally weird that he read my expression but totally sweet that he knew how to handle the situation. Although Indie would never purposely harm anyone, his gigantic head has gotten him into trouble more times than I can count. I had to visit the dentist bright and early one Saturday morning several years ago on account of Indie's fortified jaw meeting my two front teeth, all because he was happy to see me. I rolled my tongue over my teeth, remembering the way it felt spitting out my own shattered pieces of enamel.

As Eleanor and Mable started walking away I absent mindedly reached out to Edward and said "thank you" as my hand fell gently on his forearm.

"I'll catch you later, Polar Bear," he said smiling as he walked away. Something about the way he said 'polar bear' was comforting. Not in a romantic way, but in the buddy old pal kind of way. It was nice to know that I could possibly have one friend up here even if he did seem to have moments of bipolar disorder. Edward seemed so normal when he wasn't under the presence of his aunt.

****

It was such a relaxed feeling in the barn the rest of the weekend. I knew my duties that needed to be accomplished and I was always one to be on time or a tad early. When I realized Arthur wasn't returning anytime soon Sunday evening I suggested to

Gertrude that we go ahead and feed his horses for him that night. She certainly wasn't thrilled but reluctantly helped me out anyway. It wasn't until about seven o'clock that night that we heard Arthur's vehicle pulling in the driveway.

I just happened to be standing near the front barn door and saw him staggering into the aisleway, the wrong aisleway mind you. His side was the other side. What on earth was he doing?

"Hey ladies!" he said all too loud and slurred. Oh my. The man was completely drunk. And he had the indecency to drive home and to be late on top of all that? He is so lucky Ms. Arnot isn't here. What am I saying? I'm sure she would overlook it anyway and tell me to take care of his horses so he could rest. I guess it is a good thing she isn't here after all.

Gertrude just giggled at his happy-go-lucky non-Arthur type attitude. I just shook my head and gently guided him to the other side and into his own bedroom. With a slight shove I told Arthur not to come out until morning and that he better not be late because there was no way I was going to cover for him. I didn't even step foot over the threshold, I just slammed the door and started back down the aisle.

"Was that Arthur you were talking to just now?" Fantastic. Edward had caught me leaving Arthur's room. Think, Dana, think. I'm not one to be a tattle tale but I had no idea how to cover this up.

"Um, yes, that is his room," I answered, trying to skirt the question as well as my way past Edward.

"Is everything alright?" His eyes narrowed and he wrinkled his nose as he turned watching me walk away. That was one thing I could not cover up—that pungent smell of alcohol. I stopped and slowly turned back around. He continued sniffing the air, walking up to me. "Is that what I think it is?"

"If you're thinking it's a lonely man, lost in a world full of beautiful women and no one to pine over but himself, then yes." I ended with a cheesy grin and noticed a sly smile crack on his slightly scruffy face. He's always been so clean shaven. This look made him much more back woodsman, without that creepy he's-going-to-chop-my-head-off-with-an-axe feeling.

"The horses have all been taken care of this evening so there is nothing to worry about. Gertrude and I have enjoyed the peace and quiet and were more than happy to see to any business that was left unfinished." That might have been all but saying "we took care of Arthur's mess," but I also wanted Edward to know that the horses were all safe and healthy. I tried not to sound defiant and the look on Edward's face seemed to capture the fact that I was trying to be sincere and honest.

"I appreciate it. Look ...." he hesitated. "I'm not sure, well I'm not sure we should even be having this conversation right here...."

"What? Talking about Arthur?" I asked, completely puzzled. Goodness, I didn't realize he had become such a god in this barn that we couldn't even talk about him anymore. I was ready to add, "the golden child and chosen one who can obviously do no wrong," but I stopped short, letting the heat build up inside me.

"Then I best be on my way. I'm not looking for trouble here, or so I thought I wasn't looking for trouble. Apparently it has found me anyway." Uh oh. It was coming and I was about to blow.

"Oh, no. This has nothing to do with Arthur." He shyly looked down at the ground while clueless me looked down as well, trying to find the answer on the cleanly swept floor.

Side note: you could totally eat off those floors if you had to. I spent a good forty-five minutes sweeping and cleaning them today. They were so clean that when I accidentally dropped my half-eaten apple and it rolled three feet I picked it up, noticed not a speck of dust on the white flesh, and finished eating it before giving the core to Indie.

We both looked up at the same time, those handsome eyes meeting mine and for a brief moment of teenage weakness, I lost my breath. Feeling uncomfortable in the silence I did what I do best. I grew impatient with waiting and I walked away. But not without first saying, "We can talk some other time then. You know where I live."

Chapter Seven

Poor Arthur was dragging Monday morning. I'm not sure what he had been drinking but it was certainly powerful stuff. I was satisfied to see that Ms. Arnot was watching him closely. Even if Edward hadn't told her what he had witnessed the night before, you had to be a fool to think nothing happened to him over the weekend.

My satisfaction quickly turned to horror as I thought that possibly this circumstance would mean more pity for Arthur; give him the day off and let Dana do all the work. I started mentally working on my defense.

Today was our first group lesson on Ms. Arnot's personal horses. She personally selected our horses and I was glad to be given Wilhelm. He was a seven-year-old Hanoverian out of Weltmeyer. He was also the youngest and most inexperienced horse she had but I felt privileged to be selected as his rider. I'm not sure if her intention was to belittle me more by giving me a hot headed W-line personality for a horse or to show what a strong rider I had proven to be at the farm. Either way I was thrilled for the opportunity.

Gertrude was given a fifteen-year-old Oldenburg schoolmaster and Arthur was using a ten-year-old Dutch mare. Although as mere individuals the three of us had completely opposite personalities when it came to day-to-day living, put us all on horseback and we actually worked well as a team. We all wanted our time to shine but we all were respectful and took turns in that spotlight.

I quickly discovered my horse knew about as much as Indie did so I was comfortable with the learning level. We worked on passage and tempi changes, getting the feel of the different styles of riding.

"If you can train the movements you need to know on a strange horse then working yours will be simplistic." It was Ms. Arnot's way of saying if you can't do it on a schoolmaster then forget about teaching your own horse.

I could see Gertrude struggling with her horse. He wasn't being disobedient but she just didn't seem to understand how to use her aids. After a few moments Ms. Arnot asked Gertrude to dismount so that she could show her what the horse needed to do. Gertrude was crushed and it broke my heart seeing her so disappointed in herself, but I knew she would get over it as soon as she was back on her own perfectly trained mare.

The lesson finished with much accomplished in my opinion. But I was starting to feel unsatisfied with my training. I know I am learning a lot and I can already see some of that improvement in me as well as in Indie. But I felt I wasn't doing good enough. I maybe wasn't improving fast enough. I never realized that positive reinforcement went such a long way, and right now I wasn't getting those helpful comments.

I mean, I know how to use it in my classroom, and I occasionally remember to use it on Indie when he does something good, but when I wasn't hearing it applied to me it started to drain me a bit. I was constantly sending up prayers asking God to show me that strength and I know He heard me, but I was starting to lose that enthusiasm. I was so looking forward to that enthusiasm carrying me through my three-month stay. Instead, I was starting to feel disheartened.

****

The week passed by with no real changes. I finally got Indie perfected on a skill we have been working on for over a year now. That was thrilling to me, but no one shared in my excitement. I ended up calling home Friday night, telling my sister all the wonderful things that were happening, trying to hide the fact that what I really wanted to do was pack up my horse and come home. I knew I couldn't hide my feelings from her and although I didn't tell her of my miseries she prayed with me over the phone and encouraged me to press on. That's what she does best. She always has the right words to say to me when I am struggling and suffering in silence.

I cried that night before bed. Gertrude was outside on the phone so I knew my tears had a time frame. I let them loose, holding a box of tissues to capture any evidence of wetness. I had a brief pity party for myself even though I knew it was wrong. I felt I deserved some pity, even if it only came from myself. I was starting to wear down physically and mentally, even to the point of buying a case of energy drinks at the local grocery store just to get me to, and through, my evening lessons on Indie.

My pity party ended short when I heard the door open. Thankfully I had already stopped crying, more confused with my situation than sadden by at that point. I threw on a quick smile and headed over to the kitchen table where Gertrude was sitting. She looked exhausted as well.

"Everything okay?" I asked, truly concerned for her welfare.

"Oh, everything's fine," she returned. "I don't think I'm cut out for this intensity of training though. I really thought it'd be easier. How do you do it?"

"How do I do what?" I asked.

"How do you do this every day, not just here but at home as

well? You must be dead by the time the day is over. Is that why you don't have anyone? I mean, not that it's any of my business but I'm curious."

Well this was a deep conversation that I never thought would happen between the two of us. The funny thing was that even with her blatantly personal question I wasn't offended or upset. As a matter of fact I felt a new source of energy as I started to give my answer.

"I love what I do, just being around the horses, keeping them happy, finding my own satisfaction in training and schooling my own horses. I've been doing this since I was a little girl and it's all I know. I honestly don't know what I would do without them. My life would be unfulfilled without God's little blessings in my barn." I paused to let that sink in first before continuing.

"Why do you call them blessings?" she asked.

"Well, for the most part everyone in my barn is there for a reason. I truly believe that God sent them there so that we could all become part of a bigger picture. I find joy being around them and hopefully they can find joy and peace when they are at their home away from home, so to speak. Most of the boarders at my barn use it as an escape, whether it be from work, family, or just from everyday reality. Some even have their horses just as pets, not even to ride at all!" This last statement made Gertrude's brows raise.

"Wow, it sounds so wonderful where you are from!" she exclaimed, making it sound like I was from some far away galaxy that was unattainable to a regular earthling. Before I could tell her she could have that same feeling too, she broke through my thoughts.

"Is that why you don't have anyone?"

So this might be a little tougher to answer but I gave it my best.

"Until I find someone who can respect my passion for horses I have no reason to force a relationship with someone who can't understand my lifestyle." Hopefully that was clear.

"But aren't you lonely?" Concern showed in her eyes as she asked. Kids these days just don't understand the true meaning of a relationship.

"I have my sister, my boarders, my co-workers and my horses to keep me company. Until the right one comes along I'm not willing to compromise for Mr. Right Now." But, there were times of loneliness. Those times were filled with prayers asking for strength and comfort. But Gertrude didn't need to know every detail. I didn't know how she was on her faith and I didn't want to push it. We'd have plenty of time for that now that the proverbial door was opened.

"Thanks, Dana. I needed to hear that."

I suddenly felt guilty for having a pity party for myself earlier. All this time I had been looking for some type of recognition from Ms. Arnot only to find that wasn't what I needed. I needed this rich, spoiled, sweetheart of a girl from New Hampshire to get me back on track.

I fell asleep instantly after my prayers that night, thanking God for sending Gertrude to me and for allowing me to be open and honest with her during our brief but meaningful talk. I think I even slept the whole night with a smile on my face, reliving the fulfillment I felt at being able to help someone else. Oh, the small joys that make me happy.

****

The weekend came again with Arthur nowhere to be found

both Saturday and Sunday night. Gertrude and I decided we would just pencil in his horses on our weekly schedule from here on out. We started to pretend that he flew off to a secret island on his private jet, where he swam and frolicked with Champagne sipping horses. So it was a bit over the top but it boosted both of our imaginations and we got a kick out of how we could make the story even more interesting.

After finishing our feedings on Sunday, we both headed back to our room for our own dinner. Gertrude and I had just gone grocery shopping so we had a few different options for food that night. I even broke down and bought some peanut butter blast chocolate ice cream for a treat. Gertrude protested, saying she would pack on the pounds if she ate any of it, but I felt we deserved a little extra motivation for all the hard work we were putting in on the weekends.

I was surprised to see a note taped to our door with my name on it. We both looked at each other and then looked up and down the barn aisle as if we would catch the person who left the message.

It was a bit of chicken scratch but I could still read it. Hey, if I can read a first-grader's handwriting I could certainly read this. It was short and to the point:

Dana,

Would you please meet me in the office when you are finished up with the horses for the evening.

Edward

"You might as well start dinner without me. I'll take care of this now and be back as soon as I'm done," I said, the note still in my hand. "Oh, and you better save me some of that ice cream. I'm sure I'll need it once I get back." I winked, knowing how much she really wanted to dig into the gallon. She just rolled her eyes, laughing.

I decided to make a quick pit stop at the bathroom to wash up. I wasn't sure how quick this little meeting was going to be so I dusted myself off with my hands, not wanting to look like a complete bum. I didn't feel the need to change. After all, this was a barn and I was there to work horses. No one ever said horses were clean animals.

I walked to the other side of the barn and approached the "Office" door with a bit of hesitation. Was Ms. Arnot going to be part of this little meeting? Should I have brought Gertrude with me as a buffer for whatever I might need a buffer for? Maybe I should have changed. I started to get whiffs of myself and they weren't pleasant.

Before knocking on the office door I took a deep breath. Here we go.

"Come in," Edward invited with a warm smile seconds after I knocked on the door. "I was just getting ready to grab a drink. Would you like anything?" A tall glass of water perhaps to wash down all this *cotton mouth* I was suddenly feeling.

"No thanks. Gertrude and I were just getting ready for dinner." I noticed that Edward wasn't overdressed for the occasion. He still had on his own work clothes — a blue and white buttoned down plaid shirt with rolled up sleeves, slightly ripped and worn out jeans, messy hair with that scruffy face that I was growing more accustomed to on the weekends. I felt a bit self-conscious but reminded myself that we were there for the same purpose: horses.

"I'm sorry to disrupt your evening but I felt that I need to share something with you although you seem to be doing fine without any explanation." Okay, now he was confusing me. My brain can't take all these riddles and guessing games. I'm a black-

and-white kind of person. Again, the awkward silence that I have no patience for filled the air.

"I'm sorry. I guess I'm not following your story." Enough shenanigans already. Get to the point because dinner and ice cream are screaming out my name right now.

"Contrary to popular belief my aunt really admires your work with your horse but feels that you haven't earned his full talents as of yet." He talked as if he wasn't used to confrontation in his job. I wonder what he did before he became manager for his aunt. Perhaps he was a low-life with no education and lived in the back of his car until finding the meaning of life. Oh shoot. He just said something and I was totally lost in my own thought.

"Wait," I broke into his sentence. "Did your aunt ask you to talk to me and make excuses for what has been happening here since we all arrived?" My boldness was shocking even me at that point. I think Edward was a bit shocked as well because his face started turning a different shade of pink.

"Well, um, being the manager I do have discussions with the head trainer about her students," he replied. He was desperately trying to sound professional but was falling short.

"In that case, if you're not expanding my work load or asking me to go back home I'm going back to my room to have a nice relaxing dinner with my roommate." I paused just in case I was going to be asked to leave or given more horses, but nothing came except a defeated sigh from Edward. I knew there was more he wanted to say but he couldn't seem to find the right words apparently. I knew walking out would be rude and I wasn't trying to upset anyone.

So before heading out I made the effort to look him in the eyes and kindly, oh so kindly, use my words nicely.

"If there is anything else you need from me you know where

I live," I tried to smile. Noticing what seemed to be his crushed spirit, I added, "And thank you, for trying to help me out," which was what I thought he was trying to do but who knows. I continued to smile as I turned and headed out the door.

On the quick walk back to my room I tried to process what just happened but ended up with nothing. Ms. Arnot liked me but didn't think I was good enough to ride with the big kids? Or possibly she thought I was enjoying my work and thought giving me more would make me happier? Or better yet, she was secretly going to kidnap my horse and have her little minions stage a freak 'accident' as an excuse for finding my remains hidden deep in the woods? Curse that overactive imagination of mine.

A sharp noise broke my deluge of questions and I suddenly stopped in my tracks. I waited a moment before I moved, listening for any other sounds that weren't horse-related. Nothing came. Not even Edward or Gertrude.

I quickly made my way back over to my side of the barn just in time to see a shadow of a figure running out the side door of the barn. I froze in my tracks before realizing I needed to run after them. It wasn't quite dark outside but the overcast skies made it somewhat difficult to find anything once I got outside the barn. I stood still, straining my eyes, hoping to find something.

But I saw nothing. Then it dawned on me. If this stranger was in such a hurry to leave what kind of trouble was the person causing in the barn. I quickly ran back inside and frantically started checking all the horses.

At some point Edward came out of the office, perhaps getting ready to head home, and saw me scurrying through the barn.

"What's going on?" he asked, making his way over to the tack room I had just entered.

"Someone was here," I replied.

"What do you mean?" He seamed quite alarmed from the panic that overtook his face.

"I heard a noise after leaving the office and saw someone running out of the barn. The person headed toward the woods but then I lost track of the sound." I continued looking through everyone's tack boxes to see if anything had been stolen.

"The horses are fine," I started to say, but as I turned around, I noticed Edward was already gone.

Chapter Eight

Sunday morning when the alarm went off I awoke with a slight headache. We had quite the storm during the night and I think some weird Canadian barometric pressure was messing with my sinuses. After checking and double checking all the horses the night before, I finally went back to the room to share my information with Gertrude. It was nice to hear the first words out of her mouth were concern for her horse.

I had reassured her everything was in place and none of the horses seemed distressed. Honestly, I was worried all night about them. What if this stranger drugged one of the horses? I was anxious to get going and hopefully find nothing out of the ordinary.

I never saw Edward again the previous night. After he took off, presumably looking for the shadow, he must have gone home. I made sure all the doors were closed and had left a multitude of lights on overnight. I couldn't care less about the electric bill. I was more concerned for Gertrude and myself, alone in a barn with a shadowy figure lingering around.

I popped some aspirin with breakfast and changed into my work clothes. Strangely enough Gertrude and I had become well-acquainted with each other, enough to not feel the need to go into the bathroom every time we needed to change clothes. We were both girls and neither of us minded. As long as we didn't parade around before putting on our clothes we were good.

I took my time feeding and cleaning the horses in the morning, paying close attention to any little detail that wasn't normal. It was a quiet day. Even the horses must have been feeling the repercussions of the weather.

A multitude of questions kept flowing through my brain all morning long. Every question was about why the shadowy figure was there and what the person did or took. Nothing was out of place. Nothing was missing. Not even a bag of grain had been stolen. It just didn't make sense to me. But I was on high alert and wondered if Edward would tell Ms. Arnot about what happened.

****

The next couple of days were quiet. Arthur was quiet as well. Those weekends must really be catching up with him. I wonder if he'll get the hint and come to his senses. Probably not. It had been a few days since my encounter with Edward and the shadow, and I hadn't seen either of them since. Edward had been keeping a low profile and that was fine with me. The fewer awkward situations the better.

If Edward had told Ms. Arnot about the encounter with the shadowy figure she certainly didn't let on. She went about her business as usual, always seemingly expecting more and more from us, well, me at least.

I had just walked out the door of our room Wednesday morning when I heard the beeping back-up sensors of a big truck. I didn't know of any delivery that was coming that day so I hurried down the aisle and out to where I heard the noise.

Anabella was outside with what appeared to be a dump truck load of gravel, presumably for the driveway. Her voice sounded strained as she raised it over the sound of the diesel engine, apparently trying to tell him where he could dump the load. I noticed that he was parked in front of the horse trailers and only briefly had to remind myself of the ignorance of non-horse people.

Anabella was doing her best to try to stay calm when all of a sudden I heard a barrage of what I could only assume was German profanity. Her arms were in full swing, showing the truck driver where to pull his truck and clearly showing where he was currently at was not acceptable. I was guessing her German dialogue was telling him exactly where she would like to see him put his loud, beeping truck. Literally.

I wasn't sure what I could do but I thought two of us would be better than one so I headed across the driveway to stand at Anabella's side. Perhaps a fresh face, not one full of such anger and frustration would help the situation. I walked over, only glancing at Anabella before addressing the driver with a smile. The truck driver did not look very friendly and instantly my attitude changed from wanting to be helpful to wanting to learn Anabella's appropriate sting of German dialogue.

"I'm sorry sir," I started, "but for safety reasons the area in front of the trailers needs to stay clear, in case of an emergency." Maybe some reasoning would help.

"Hey, it's not my worry where it goes. I'm not in charge of spreading the stuff. You ordered it, you spread it," he replied gruffly. He was grubby looking, maybe missing a few showers (and a few teeth).

"Listen, I haul a forty-foot trailer for a living, with live animals, not just rock. If it's too hard for you to move your truck why don't you get down and just let me do it." It wasn't a question, more like an inappropriate statement. Oh great, here comes the bitter. Man, I am trying so hard to stay clean while I am here. Then I started to worry because I saw the driver start to get down from his truck. Even Anabella took a step back, not willing to stand up for me as I was for her.

"You're late," came a voice from behind me. Thank goodness Edward showed up, although I was handling the situation, I think. Edward had a look of seriousness across his face and I realized the truck driver was, in all actuality, late. The look on the truck driver's face was priceless. He went from hard and gruff to meek and timid with one short breath. I stood back in amazement, wondering for the millionth time why men were more respected by other men than women were. So much for fairness and equality.

"I'm sorry," replied the trucker. "We were down a truck and had to rearrange some of our deliveries."

"Well, now. That looks like your problem, not mine. I expected this yesterday when I was told and now I'm a day behind. I'll be talking to the manager as soon as I get back to the office. Please take your truck and dump it on the east side of the barn." And with that, Edward turned, catching my eye, winked, and walked back to the barn.

I so desperately wanted to ask him about the shadowy figure, but he was a man on a mission and I couldn't bring myself to stop him with foolish questions. What I really wanted to know was if he told his aunt. Man, was I nosy or what?

I watched the truck driver slink back into his cab and move the truck where he was told. Seriously? I need to learn the art of bossing people around. So much more can get accomplished in my day that way.

As I was walking back to the barn I suddenly realized Anabella was nowhere to be found. How did she disappear so quickly and when did she leave me? Another skill I need to learn: how to be stealthy. My list was getting terribly long and not in a good way. These Canadians were good — real good — at disappearing.

Back in the barn Gertrude popped her head out of the stall she was cleaning when I came back in from the gravel incident.

"What was going on out there?" she asked in a quiet voice, not knowing exactly where Anabella was in the barn.

"Did you hear her?" I asked but then continued on without her answer. "I've never seen her so full of emotion. I certainly couldn't help her either. That man couldn't care less what we said, but boy, when Edward showed up he just about groveled at his feet with an apology. And not an apology toward me and Anabella of course, but for the fact that he was a day late with the delivery." I had to catch my breath because I had just spit all that out without coming up for air.

"Wow," was all Gertrude could say.

"Yeah, but now I'm wondering why we weren't told about this. I mean, we have a schedule for everything else including grain delivery. Why wasn't this on the list?" I could see Gertrude really didn't feel as deeply about the matter as I did.

I pondered that thought as I walked to get my wheelbarrow and pick. I thought the driveway looked just fine and couldn't quite figure out where all that rock was needed. I had to remind myself that it really was none of my business. This was just a temporary job for me so that I could improve my riding style and my training aids. What they did with their facility was totally up to them. Of course, I'm sure they would like that I had given my stamp of approval.

That day we were having another group lesson. We hadn't been told what horses we were going to be riding but I assumed they would be the same ones. I had already started to bond with Wilhelm and was learning that he was an awful lot like Indie in regards to his abilities and mind-set. I had already changed into my riding clothes and headed to Whil's stall when I saw Arthur walking down the aisle toward me.

"Hey, Arty." I knew he didn't like the nickname, but come on. We'd been working together almost every day (with the exception of the weekends he came home drunk or didn't come home at all) for the past month so it was only fitting that it start being used on a regular basis.

"Very funny, princess," he said in a tone that would only be acceptable coming from him. "I get Wilhem today. Amy's in the office with new horses for today's ride. You best see who you'll be riding before you get in trouble or punished." This man was truly amazing. He could say something so offensive and hurtful with such a straight face but yet I never could seem offended or hurt when he said it with that type of inflection.

"Thanks," I offered as I half-walked, half-trotted to the office. The door was wide open and I could clearly see Ms. Arnot at her desk, reading glasses hanging off the bridge of her nose. She looked up when I knocked and then motioned me to come on in. She didn't offer a seat so I didn't take one. I knew I would be in a hurry to get my horse ready, whichever she had chosen for me that day.

"I gave Wilhelm to Arthur today to see how well you've trained him," she started and paused. I replayed her comment in my mind and had to silently chuckle because I had to assume she was talking about the horse. I gave a short nod, waiting for her to continue.

Oh, no. What if I were to sit this lesson out? If I wasn't good enough to ride the young horse what would she put me on? Some crotchety old school master? Well, I could learn from a schoolmaster as well. My overactive mind was jumping around like a professional game of ping-pong.

"Anabella will show you where all Rinaldi's tack is. I expect to see professionalism, courtesy, and respect not only for the horse but for other riders as well. Do we have an understanding?" Do I understand what has just been asked of me? Of course not. Where did this come from? Am I still breathing? Then I realized she still needed an answer.

"Of course," I said and quickly added, "and thank you so much." There wasn't time for more words because the look she gave me made me feel like I was already running late for my lesson.

I was elated, excited, scared, worried, shocked, and terrified all in the few steps it took to get to Rinaldi's tack locker which was where I found Anabella waiting for me. There was no change in her facial expression so I was unable to tell if she was upset with me or really didn't care who got to ride the horse. I couldn't spend time worrying about it with time ticking away as it was.

Anabella and I had never had a real conversation since my arrival and it appeared we wouldn't be having one that day either. She showed me his locker and where to find his saddle pad and wraps before exiting to finish her own work for the day.

I quickly grabbed the Bates saddle, double bridle, grooming box, whip, and sugar cube as instructed. I'd come back for the gray and black saddle pad with matching black polo wraps in a minute. This is going to be awesome! I wish someone had a camera to take a picture of this once in a lifetime opportunity I am about to have. I wonder if Arthur or Gertrude know what is going on with the switch. I hope they won't be upset with me about the change. It's not like I ever asked Ms. Arnot to ride her personal show horse.

Her personal show horse. Rinaldi. Silver medal winner at the World Equestrian Games. What if something happens to him while I'm riding? What if I totally bomb this opportunity? Seriously, Dana? Why do I have to ask myself so many questions?

Tacking up Rinaldi I talked myself into thinking that this was just another horse. Come on. What made him so different than Indie besides his color and his owner? Any good horse in the right hands could become something wonderful and famous with the potential to represent his country. After all, that was my reason for coming here. I didn't really expect to be riding her horse but I certainly wasn't going to pass up the opportunity.

Rinaldi seemed quiet and polite as I got him ready and led him into the arena. His ground manners were superb and I had hoped those same manners would transfer to the saddle as well. Gertrude and Arthur were already in the arena warming up and I didn't have the heart to look at either one of them. I knew at some point during our forty-five minute lesson I would have to encounter them, but I took my chances in hoping we would always be at opposite ends of the arena.

As we rode, I could tell Rinaldi was starting to get fired up. I mentally reminded myself to take deep breaths, use my half halts, and pray that all would work on my behalf. All eyes, for the most part, were on me and Rinaldi, and my massive steed was starting to take matters into his own hooves. I could feel the muscles in my arms start to engage and I tried to keep a firm but relaxed seat. I knew not to brace my body for fear that Rinaldi would get the wrong impression and become confused and frustrated at my lack of proper aids. He was ready to put on a show and Ms. Arnot knew it.

It's true. All upper-level dressage horses, as calm as they may appear to the audience, have that fire just waiting to explode at any moment. The true talent comes from the rider, showing the calm ability to contain that fire and release it all at the right moments during the ride. I knew those moments and hoped that I could utilize my talents on the beast.

To my surprise, and Ms. Arnot's I would imagine, Rinaldi proved to be a gentleman and respected my aids and waited for my signals. It was amazing to feel all that power contained underneath my little leather saddle. Indie certainly had the power, he was just not physically mature enough to know how to contain it when asked.

Our lesson finished quite successfully if you ask me. I learned a lot, not just about how to ask for certain movements, but about myself as well. I said a silent prayer as I dismounted Rinaldi, thanking God for giving me that strength that I'm always asking for on a daily basis. It wasn't even a physical strength so much as a mental attitude on how to really appreciate the skills and talents of both horse and rider.

I was so excited over our delightful ride that it was hard to wipe the smile off my face. I could tell that Arthur would have been more than happy to wipe if off for me, but I wasn't going to let him steal my joy. I also wasn't going to gloat in his face, although I wanted to so desperately. I decided to steer clear of him for most of the afternoon just in case I couldn't control myself, or vice versa.

In all honesty, I really didn't watch the other two riding. I was so focused on what I needed to do that I did not take the time to enjoy my riding mates and their new mounts. Feeling bad about that I walked over to Gertrude after I was finished cooling and detacking Rinaldi to see what she thought about her ride.

"So how was, um," shoot! I couldn't think of her horse's name. I fumbled a bit, trying to look at a halter or something that might have had his name on it but came up short.

"Prince," she finished, seeing how I was struggling. I couldn't quite read her expression. Was she upset with me, or was she just exhausted from the ride? I went with exhausted and continued my conversation.

"He's beautiful. How did you like riding him?" I asked.

"He's no Jasmine, that's for sure. I think I'm partial to mares." In my opinion I think she's just partial to schoolmasters but hey, who am I to judge?

"He didn't really listen to me and I was kind of getting frustrated with him. I don't know, maybe I'm just not cut out to be a trainer." Whoa there, sunshine. Is that why she is really here? She wants to be a trainer? I tried to hide my astonishment by keeping the rest of our small talk very small.

"Well, at least you get the opportunity to see what you like and what you don't enjoy as much. That will definitely help you in the long run when it comes to selecting horses to train." Was that really true, though? Ending our chit chat I casually threw in our dinner plans.

"You go wash up. I'll defrost us something for dinner," I smiled.

"Thanks, but I already have plans for dinner. Edward and I are meeting for dinner this evening." Astonished again, this time it was not hidden at all. I felt all the color being sucked out of my frozen expression.

Chapter Nine

Sleep did not come easily that night. I was emotionally torn, elated from my ride, and yet something else was nagging at me. I couldn't put my finger on it though. I wasn't hurt. I wasn't disappointed. Perhaps I was just living in a perfect bubble of happiness and thought things were just perfect the way they were in Canada. I guess I felt a bit betrayed even though I really didn't care what Gertrude and Edward did that night. No really, I didn't care. In two months we would all be going our separate ways and would probably never see each other again. And that was fine with me. I'm not one for attachments.

I finally rested on the thought that I was the first one privileged to ride Rinaldi and did a fine job at that. I started wondering if I would be given any more opportunities to ride him again during my stay and thought it might be a good idea to talk to Ms. Arnot the next day to thank her again. I didn't want to push my luck but I wanted her to know that I truly enjoyed myself. With that, I drifted off to a restful sleep.

****

The next morning I was ready to get to work, finding Ms. Arnot and hoping to have made a good impression the day before. I got up quietly as usual, as not to wake Gertrude too quickly. I've learned her morning routine and knew how not to disturb her. I was shocked when I noticed her bed was empty.

Was I really going to have to deal with this for the rest of the summer? I tried not to be presumptuous, but come on. A date with a really hot guy? What would her poor boyfriend think of all this?

No. I refuse to let my mind go there. Maybe she was already up and feeding the horses. I was soon going to find out. I gobbled down my breakfast and threw on my nasty, dirty barn jeans that had not been washed since my arrival. They were starting to smell funky but I didn't care.

In the aisleway all was calm until the horses heard my footsteps. Nickers of delight and greed sounded throughout the barn, confirming the fact that Gertrude had not yet made it into the barn to feed. I let out an audible sigh as I walked to the hay room to start feeding.

It wasn't until about fifteen minutes later that Gertrude magically showed up in the barn to help. I didn't want to be nosy nor did I want to look upset that she didn't come home the night before. I'm sure she didn't want me acting like her mother and I certainly wasn't willing to take on that role, although perhaps she needed one right now.

"Morning," I said as lightly as possible as she walked past the stall I was cleaning.

"Oh, good morning." She seemed happy and I couldn't be upset with her. After a disappointing ride the day before she apparently found something to lift her spirits. Who was I to crush her happiness?

"Thanks for feeding my horses. I totally slept in this morning." She hung around my stall, not making a whole lot of attempt to get started on her own stalls. Was she trying to get me to ask her what went on the night before?

"No problem," I responded. "I wasn't quite sure if you had already fed yet since I didn't see you this morning." There it was.

I opened the door and quickly wanted to slam it shut it again, but it was too late. I saw a smile beam across Gertrude's face and suddenly felt like a teenager back in high school. I'm too old for this foolishness.

Before Gertrude had time to divulge her exciting details about the previous night, Arthur appeared around the corner. Argh, it was too early for this.

"Hey, sweeties," he called out, drawing out the word "sweeties" in his very unmasculine voice. Gertrude giggled while puzzlement once again appeared on my face. What was with all the chipper attitudes this morning? Am I the only one trying to get work done?

"I'm making some super strong coffee. Does anyone else need one besides me and Trudie?" Seeing that I was the only other one out there I responded with a polite, "no thanks."

Did he just call Gertrude 'Trudie'? I was so totally missing something but then thought that sometimes it was best to stay in the dark, especially with those two. I was still focusing on my talk later that day with Ms. Arnot. I wanted a clear head, not one all hyped up on caffeine and stories of unbecoming roommate behaviors.

"Suit yourself, princess," he said over his shoulder as he whisked himself down the aisle to the lounge where the coffee maker was apparently brewing with some 'super strong' coffee. Ugh. Trudie was two steps behind him, giggling as she talked in a low but girly voice. And all this time I thought Gertrude and I were allies. Boy how the tides do turn. I suddenly felt like an outsider, not fitting in with the gang and being ousted from the group due to my cultural and moral differences.

My thought of being a good Christian witness to these people started to fizzle. I needed to do something that would show them the good in this world and how the only true happiness came when you came to know Christ. I felt my opportunity to witness had just come and gone as quickly as the clean sawdust in my stalls. Instead of asking what I could do to change things I started letting my mind wander off into the woods, literally.

When I get down on myself I sometimes let my mind wander off to a better place, one in which I find comfort and peace. The woods back home are where I have my cross-country course, designed solely for my enjoyment away from the dressage ring. For fun, I take my trusty gray mare out there and jump the natural wonders provided in the fallen logs, watery ditches, and multi-leveled banks. It's my first love when it comes to riding horses and I will always keep a piece of that with me.

I started thinking of all that I was missing back home that summer. All the ride times with my sister and all our fun cross country trail adventures. Early mornings trying to beat the sun on the back ring. Cool rides under the shade of the tall trees. Peace and quiet of not having to deal with juveniles and their daily drama. I smiled to myself, reminded of the wonderful opportunity I have here and the one-time shot I have to learn as much as I can to make a good impression.

I said a silent prayer, one of many throughout my regular day. I not only prayed for my family but I prayed for myself. For the courage to stand up for what I believe in and to be brave during confrontation. I have a tendency of becoming too defensive which in turn leads to some pretty nasty hurt feelings on both ends. I don't want that here. I want to be the light and I want to shine, not be covered by the compromising atmosphere.

I decided that I would finally break out the iPod and take a brief run through the trails later that evening after night checks. It would still be light and I could use the refresher. My goal was actually to run every night while I was there but for the most part I was too exhausted at the end of the day and looked forward to a shower and cozy early bedtime. That night though, I needed a change of pace. Something needed to change, not only in my attitude but my whole entire mental state.

I'd pretty much finished with all my horses after that long thought process and found that Arthur and Gertrude were still busy working on their stalls. I cleaned up my stuff and headed to my bathroom to wash up before a quick lunch. I figured Trudie already had plans with Arthur so I decided not to wait for her that day. I also decided not to help her. Not because I didn't want to but because I didn't want to hear her constant jabber. I was bound to hear about it later that night anyway.

As soon as I walked out of the bathroom I was greeted by our clean-shaven barn manager, apparently waiting for me, foot propped up against the side of the barn directly across from the bathroom door. I thought it a tad weird that someone was waiting for me right outside the bathroom and then suddenly felt self-conscious. Did I make any inappropriate noises while in there? I told myself it was too bad if I did. It is a bathroom after all and if you're going to be lingering outside the door then you should be the one feeling embarrassed right now, not me.

"Hey, what's up?" I asked casually, wiping my clean hands on my filthy jeans. I hoped I wasn't going to get his version of what happened the night before. It really wasn't necessary or even something I was looking forward to at that moment. I just really wanted lunch. Maybe, to make it exciting, I would even add some dessert. And perhaps find some giant cotton balls to shove in my ears for later that night when Gertrude and I had our alone time.

"Amy would like to see you in her office," was his response.

Someone apparently flipped the mood switch, again.

"Okay, you mean now?" Silly question but I was looking to be amused.

"Please, I'll walk you over."

Really? Do I look like I just arrived? I know where the office is. I so desperately tried to stifle a laugh but it must have been more audible than I had anticipated.

"Something funny?" he questioned innocently, those eyes playing their pity on me.

"Um, yeah. I think I can find the office on my own," I replied, an ever so slight hint of smirky sarcasm.

Of course, he looked crushed, again, but this time I wasn't falling for it. I just kept on walking to the other side of the barn and threw back a "thanks!" before rounding the corner. Thankfully, he didn't follow.

The office door was closed so I knocked and waited to be invited in for my lashing, I mean my talk.

Oh no, my talk. My mind started fumbling for the right words in the right order that I had practiced over and over in my head. I had been thinking of this talk all last night and all day, about how wonderful I am, I mean the ride was, and how grateful she should be, I mean I was, for riding her horse. Oh fantastic. Perhaps I'll just keep my mouth shut this time.

I walked into the office and sat down in one of the chairs, but not the one directly across from her. It made me feel too much like a target with a giant bull's-eye on my forehead. Ms. Arnot looked rather peaceful and satisfied with herself and that made all the muscles in my body relax, but only a little bit. I changed my mind at the last minute and thought that if I were ever going to speak up, now was the time.

"Ms. Arnot, I want to thank you again for letting me ride Rinaldi yesterday. It was such an honor." I waited. Her face seemed to bare the slightest, oh so slightest hint of a smile. Maybe it was just the lighting.

"You're velcome," she replied with her German accent. "And now I have a proposition for you," she continued.

What on earth could she possibly want from me? A liver? A kidney? Maybe some bone marrow would do the trick. I've heard it can be quite painful to give though.

"I would like to rearrange lessons this afternoon and ride Indie instead."

Instead of what? I thought to myself.

"So I would ride Indie instead of one of the school horses?" I asked, slightly confused.

Then the smile came out, for sure this time. She actually looked quite pleasant with such a wonderful smile. And it didn't look mean or vindictive in any way.

"No, I mean *I* would ride Indie this afternoon," she said, still smiling.

The color felt like it drained from my face and I fell mute, but only momentarily.

"Of, of course, I mean, that would be wonderful! I would love to see what you thought of him and what you could do for him! It would be such an honor and privilege to watch and learn with you on his back," came the mouth spewage, words coming quicker and quicker as I spoke. She finally put up a hand as if to stop me from continuing on in what was probably a painful manner for both her and me. I still saw the smile on her face which indicated she was not completely put off by my over jubilation of her offer. I took a deep breath as if to hold in the rest of my gratitude.

"It's settled then. Please have him tacked up and ready by 2 p.m. I will be looking forward to the ride." There were still no warm fuzzies between the two of us but I started to feel a bit more, oh I don't know, respect from her end, perhaps. First riding Rinaldi and now the world-class equestrian offering to get on my horse and ride, rearranging a schedule that had been set in stone since day one.

I smiled whole heartedly and stood, thanking her again before walking out the door. As I walked down the aisle I absentmindedly looked at all the barn horses. I've been working my tail off trying to earn my keep here and trying to show that I am not just anybody. I am somebody who is determined to work my way to the top, not just have it handed to me like some other people thought it should be done. I'm not trying to rip on anyone, just proving to myself that hard work, dedication, and a good heart can get you places in this world. I guess it really was my day to change.

I was still smiling when I reached my room and I didn't even care if any one saw me. Honestly, I couldn't even tell you if Arthur or Gertrude were in the barn or not. I was happy and I was proud of the fact that Ms. Arnot was seeing something, something that I didn't think she would see in us. Potential.

And it felt good.

Chapter Ten

Needless to say I had Indie out of his stall at one o'clock for fear of not being ready on time. He didn't need to be lunged and I certainly wasn't going to hand graze him before a ride. Heaven forbid he thinks he already got his treat so he doesn't have to perform for his new rider. I decided the best thing for him and me both would be a massage. Yes, I definitely needed one, but there was no time to run out and get one for myself. Instead, I pulled out a stool and started working on the large muscles in Indie's hind quarters.

I had learned equine massage many years ago and always thought about pursuing a career in the practice, but I didn't think I could actually make a living at it. So I just practiced on our own personal horses at our barn back home. It was amazing the difference you could see and feel under saddle after a really good massage.

Just like any other professional athlete, horses need to keep their muscles soft and supple for the constant demands any riding discipline puts on their bodies. So few riders take the time to see the toll that their demanding rides place on their horses. Many of the richer equestrians just sell their horses as broken and buy another one to replace and start the vicious cycle all over again. Sad.

I had Indie crosstied in the tack stall so he would be out of the aisleway. He barely fit, his nose hanging out into the aisle like a sardine being smooshed into one of those little metal cans. He was my watch dog though. If anyone was coming he would perk up his ears letting me know ahead of time as not to be so startled. I was halfway through my massage, and my train of thought, when Gertrude came over, Indie giving me ample warning that I was getting a visitor.

"He looks like he's actually enjoying that. What are you doing?" Thank you, Gertrude for helping prove my point about clueless equestrians.

"I'm massaging him. It helps release any tension in the muscles and allows the blood to flow better through his body," I tried to keep the explanation simple.

"Oh, good thing Jasmine isn't tense," was her reply. Oh, for the love of horses this girl really needs to get a clue. I kept my mouth shut and continued my work, my hands really starting to get tired. I pulled a massaging tool out of my pocket to work on some of the deeper muscle tissue. It gave my hands a chance to rest a bit before finishing.

I heard footsteps coming down the aisle and assumed it was Arthur joining our little party. Indie seemed to be getting irritated at all the intrusions during his spa time.

"There you are," came a smiling man's voice. That was no Arthur. It was Edward. I didn't see him yet since I was hidden nicely away in the tack stall, still working on Indie's hind end. Being nosy I glanced over at a beaming Gertrude as she half-walked, half-skipped over to Edward and threw her arms around him. Gag me with a spoon. Both came into sight and I could tell I caught Edward's eye. He quickly looked uncomfortable, trying so nicely to push Gertrude away. She didn't seem to mind but continued to try to hang on his arm.

"Hello, Dana," he felt obligated to state.

"Hey," was my one syllable reply. I didn't owe this man anything, nor did he owe me anything. This was a business deal, all of us being there in Canada training with Ms. Arnot. She was doing it to keep her name up with the USEF and we were doing it to use her name for our benefit in the show world. All parties were benefiting and I didn't need anything from the manager except a good report with his employer. As far as I was concerned I was doing a good job.

Edward turned his attention to Gertrude. "Let's go to the office," he suggested. Please, go, I thought to myself.

"Oh, I'd love to," she started gushing but then continued responsibly, "but I have to get ready for my lesson."

"That's what I need to talk to you about. You won't be having a lesson this afternoon but are welcome to watch Amy ride."

"How exciting! Is she riding Rinaldi? Will we be able to ask her questions during her ride?" Gertrude was so excited, literally jumping up and down in the aisleway. None of us had really watched Ms. Arnot ride her main show horse since we had started there. It took everything within me not to burst with joy, but I could tell the smile on my face was totally visible. I did try, though, to contain myself.

Edward knew the change of plans and looked over at me, hoping I would help out and fill in the blanks for dear Trudie. I just looked right back at him and shrugged my shoulders as if to say, "not my problem!" Now, I'm not one to take a lot of joy from other people's struggles but that day was an exception.

"Um," he fumbled. "She'll be riding Dana's horse today."

It wasn't quite disappointment crossing over Gertrude's face. More like confusion, and then as if she figured out the plan that quickly, she smiled again.

"I better go check with her to see when she's going to be riding Jasmine," she replied, pecking Edward on the cheek before heading to what I could only assume would be the office. It was a good question and I gave Gertrude credit for thinking that far in advance.

Edward walked over to Indie and started stroking his face in silence. Oh, this was ridiculous. I hated uncomfortable and awkward situations and didn't want to spend the rest of my time there trying to avoid certain people.

"He likes men," I offered.

"He is a beautiful animal," was Edward's reply. I didn't feel the effort in which to make conversation so I just continued on with my work, checking my watch to make sure I still had enough time. I would give myself about five more minutes and then I would start tacking him up for his debut.

Maybe I should take these next few minutes to give my tack a quick cleaning. Nah, I don't want her to think I'm anal because I'm not. Why be something I'm not.

With that thought I looked up where Edward had been petting Indie just a few moments earlier and noticed he was gone.

He would have made the effort had he wanted to fix things. But he didn't. And that was fine. I like black and white. Too much gray area hurts my head.

It took a while for me to figure out what outfit I wanted Indie to wear. He didn't have to match me and so I tried to remember what Ms. Arnot usually wears when she rides. I decided to stick with the dark gray and black tones with light gray polo wraps to accent. The dark wraps didn't show off his fantastic leg motion that stems from his Holsteiner side.

Thankfully, I was in the arena before Ms. Arnot arrived. Gertrude and Arthur were already in the viewing room, chatting away with each other and looking rather chummy. I felt the need to stay out there in the arena while the ride was taking place, not only to listen to what she had to say about my horse but just in case Indie decided a new rider was not in the plans that day.

Fortunately, Ms. Arnot arrived wearing dark gray breeches and a white polo shirt with black trim. How perfect. Now only if the ride would go as perfectly and the matching outfits.

I handed over the double reins and stepped back, grabbing the mounting block and placing it directly under the stirrup. I did have my video camera, which I hadn't even taken out of its case until about an hour before, and was prepared to multi-task—watch with my eyes while watching through the camera, listening for instructions on how to better my horse, and trying to keep my lunch down. At one point I feared I wouldn't be able to handle everything at once.

But I did. And it was great. Indie was phenomenal for Ms. Arnot. She even got him to piaffe and squeezed out a decent canter pirouette. During the ride I was told what aids were being used and how to effectively get my horse to respond without being pushy. I knew hearing it and trying it were two totally different things but I was excited anyway.

Gertrude and Arthur ended up staying for the whole ride which surprised me. I really didn't think they were interested in anything but themselves but perhaps I was wrong. Gertrude met me out in the arena after Ms. Arnot had dismounted and walked away. Arthur vanished and that was probably for the best.

"He looked great!" Gertrude praised. It seemed sincere and I was very thankful that I still possibly had a friend in Gertrude.

"Thanks! Now *I* just need to make him look like that. She sure made it look easy but I know better with him," I said, giving Indie a love tap on the ear. He looked exhausted, but happy. We headed back to our tack stall where I would hose him down to cool him off before putting him away. I would take him out later on that night, just to stretch his legs.

Gertrude had followed us like a puppy, like she was looking for something to do. I didn't mind that day. We had a good lesson and nothing could take that moment away, not for a long time. Even Arthur's self-absorbed little world. Even Edward, the sleazy barn manager. Okay, so sleazy might be a bit harsh. I still don't know the full story of last night so I shouldn't judge, again.

"What do you think of Edward?" she asked. Guess we weren't waiting for a more private moment.

"Well," I started, choosing my words wisely. "He seems kind toward the animals. He knows how to manage a good running schedule. And he is the owner's nephew so that counts for something." I left it at that to see if any of it sunk in and made sense. She didn't seem satisfied with my description.

"I know, but what do you think of him personally?" She picked up one of my brushes and started brushing out the sweat marks on Indie's back. I didn't have the heart to tell her I was going to hose him down anyway so the brushing was not necessary. I also neglected to tell her that Indie despised being groomed. It was a fate worse than death. I haven't quite figured that one out yet and in all honesty have really given up trying.

"He does have handsome good looks," I smiled at her. Again, obvious but I knew I could reach her there.

"He is really hot," she admitted. Her hesitation made me think that she was actually contemplating something, even if just briefly. Her giddy smile slowly started to fade.

"I have a boyfriend back home that I am in love with," said again with the pause. Did she think I was unaware of the constant texting to the boyfriend back home? But I let her talk it out.

"Am I cheating on him, wanting to hang out with Edward?" She looked right at me, desperately wanting a truthful answer.

So I gave it to her.

"Technically, yes. If you want to be more than friends with Edward then you need to be fair to your guy back home. Breaking up over the phone, or out of the country for that fact, is a bit harsh but you gotta do what you gotta do," I explained so professionally.

"That's what I was afraid of," Gertrude said, putting the brush back in the grooming box.

"I think I'm just lonely up here," she continued. It made sense. She seemed the type to always have someone by her side. I was a bit older and perhaps not quite immature enough for her. And then there was Arthur. She was trying so hard to be his pal.

I stopped unwrapping Indie's legs and looked at Gertrude. She was a beautiful young lady and I could see why so many people liked her, but I'm sure not always for the right reasons.

"Listen, we're only here for a short time. When summer is over and we go home is Edward going to go with you? Do you think that when you get back home your guy will gladly take you back after you had your fling up here?" Although I was pushy I was keeping my tone gentle. She needed to hear it out loud even if it was constantly nagging at the back of her mind.

"You're right. I need to talk to Edward and see what his plans are. Maybe I can figure some things out then."

Did that conversation just totally go the wrong way or what? I mentally shook my head and went back to work. Gertrude started walking away, hopefully to to straighten things out with Edward, but she stopped just a few steps later and turned around, a light bulb popping off in her head.

"I wonder if that's what he meant last night." She walked back over to me, obviously replaying the night before in her head. "After dinner we went to that giant pond up the road, you know the one? Anyway, while we were strolling the bank, he said he's really looking forward to moving on and starting his business. I thought he was just making small talk, which is not really what I wanted to do, but now that I'm thinking about it, he had other things on his mind.

"Do you think that he was trying to give me a hint? Maybe letting me know that he wasn't planning on staying up here? He really didn't return any of my advances … why would he even ask me to dinner then?"

I am not the mama hen and I am clearly not the one who should be answering these questions. What happened to the idea that I was here to work on my equestrian skills, not my people skills?

"Here's what I think," I started, perhaps a little more gruffly than anticipated. Backing off a bit with my agitated tone I continued with a kind smile. "I think you need to talk to Edward about this. I can't really tell you what you need to do or how he is feeling. That is between the two of you."

"Thanks, Dana. I tried to talk to Arthur last night but he was more interested in what he could do if he were the barn manager here. Leave it to him to think of bettering himself," she said laughing to herself. With that she started walking off again.

Last night?

"Wait!" I called out to her. "Last night? You didn't come home last night." It wasn't an accusation but now I was confused.

"Oh, I stayed in Arthur's room last night. It was late when I got back and I didn't want to wake you. I happened to see Arthur and ended up chatting with him for a while, so I just crashed there. Did you think I stayed with Edward? You're too funny." And with that she had disappeared around the corner.

Wow, how quickly I judged the two of them.

Chapter Eleven

After a nice long talk with Edward the other day, Gertrude had come to her senses. I can't say he was truly interested in her but thankfully she was wise enough to see that it just wasn't going to work out. She was happy with her guy back home and even seemed to be talking and texting more than she had in the past. I was glad to see her happy and really wanted to see that phone bill.

Edward continued to confuse me. He was able to change characters so quickly and easily that I wasn't sure I knew the real Edward. He was pretty good at his job but yet something about him made me wonder what he was really doing there. One of these days I hope to get up the nerve to ask him.

The next few days were extremely warm and it was difficult for me to do any work. Functioning in hot weather was not something I excelled at nor was my body willing to try. I did what I had to do, taking frequent breaks, drinking lots of water, and constantly checking to see the horses were doing alright as well. Thankfully they all had stall fans which really helped keep them cool. It also helped when I was in their stalls cleaning.

The weekend was supposed to be a bit cooler and slightly less humid. That was good because the three of us were going to be riding for an audience that weekend. Ms. Arnot had invited several local trainers and a few of her friends to come up to the farm to have a clinic. Those trainers would be riding their own horses but would also have an opportunity to watch us ride as well, if they so desired.

I didn't know who any of the people were but I was really hoping they would be too busy tending to their own horses that they wouldn't watch our rides. We were just a bunch of adult amateurs from the States trying to learn some pointers from our Olympic guide. Ms. Arnot had not made a big deal about the clinic but she expected us to be prompt, professional, and helpful in any way we could for her guests. Of course.

Together, Arthur, Gertrude, and I prepared five stalls for our guest horses that would be spending the weekend. They would stay with us from Friday night until Sunday morning. We also prepared three more stalls for the daily haul-ins. It was exciting to have a change of pace for once, although I could tell Arthur was going to miss his weekend drinking binge.

Trailers started pulling in around noon on Friday. I was finished with my stalls and had a brief moment to wash up and look somewhat presentable for our guests. They all had assigned stalls which was a good thing since we would be entertaining some stallions that weekend. Edward had volunteered to help out during the weekend just in case we needed some extra hands.

By four o'clock all of our out-of-town guests had arrived, including the captain of the Enterprise, you know, the Next Generation. I swear the man looked just like Captain Jean Luc Picard. I knew Arthur would get a kick out of him.

All the riders that were spending the weekend were staying in the main house. I guess I hadn't realized how big it was. We were never offered a tour at any time and I never really asked about it but was certainly curious as to how all those people, most with one other member in their party, were going to fit inside that brick ranch.

It was almost feeding time when Edward rounded us all up in the office for a quick meeting. I sat down in one of the chairs awaiting my printed schedule. When Edward passed them all out I had to take a double look. Why was my name posted as Lead? Lead what? It couldn't mean that I was in charge this weekend, could it?

"As you can see our schedule looks a bit different for this weekend," Edward started. "We will still run our regular jobs as usual, just adding the visiting horses to our list. Due to the larger amount of horses and the fact that Anabella will be out of town for the next week Amy has designated Dana as the Lead this weekend." He looked over at my shocked face and gave me the warmest smile I have ever seen. It helped ease the tension in my own face but I sat frozen, waiting for a more detailed explanation.

"Oh, good," Arthur started chirping. "Does that mean she gets to take care of all the guest horses because I really need some time off this weekend."

"Absolutely not," was Edward's stern reply. If Edward ever liked Arthur he certainly didn't make it obvious.

"All it means is that Dana will be responsible for the feeding care of the guest horses. You two will be responsible for keeping their stalls impeccable while they are here."

You could see the torment in Arthur's eyes and I knew right then and there he would be working out some sort of trade deal with Gertrude. I had to get a hold of her before he did and tell her not to take over his responsibilities.

"You are asked not to leave the property unless absolutely necessary. We have a reputation here and would ask that you show these professionals courtesy, respect, and just plain old common horse sense." Way to finally step up to that managerial title, Edward. Bravo.

"If I'm not mistaken it is feeding time. All of the riders have a schedule of their ride time," he continued as he handed out another sheet of paper. "Try to take care of the stalls while the horses are out as to avoid any confrontation. There are two stallions that I will be overseeing as well. If you need help I will be out here all weekend. I am bunking with Arthur—come get me anytime you need anything." I think that was directed at me seeing that he was staring in my direction. Oh, I will so live up to this challenge.

"Most of the riders will probably be out in the arena later this evening to get in some warm-up time." Edward walked over to the door as if to indicate it was time to leave. So like good little students we all got up and followed. "Take advantage of this weekend. You're going to see a lot of good riding, and they anticipate to see a lot of good riding from you guys, too."

No pressure. In all honesty, I would much rather be feeding all the horses by myself anyway. That way I knew they were all fed on time and received the same portions each meal. I was totally thrilled to be the Lead. I was also thrilled to see Arthur squirm at the shear thought of me having a smidgen of power over him.

I made sure I was the last one in line to leave the office. I knew I had to get feeding but I wanted to show my appreciation. I was always taught to be thankful and respectful when given a gift. This was a gift to me.

After Gertrude and Arthur had walked out the door I approached Edward.

"I'm not sure whose idea it was for this schedule but thanks." Oh, if those eyes could only follow me around forever I would be so content. Good for Gertrude for not falling under his spell.

"It was actually Amy's idea but I approved," he said with his dancing smile. "She's a hard nut to crack and I really didn't think anyone could do it, but you proved that theory wrong. There's something different about you, Dana. I can't quite put my finger on it but we still have time," he teased, I think. Time was running out and although I desperately wanted to, I wasn't about to waste any of it on him.

"I also want to make sure everything is okay, you know, here at the barn and with ... everyone," Edward continued, glancing down at his barn boots. I knew exactly what he was getting at but I wasn't going to make it easy for him.

"Oh everything is going great! I was so thrilled to see Ms. Arnot ride Indie and now being chosen as the Lead this weekend ... I couldn't ask for anything more!" was my more than chipper reply. The sarcastic smile was just beaming off my face.

Not sure how to reply, apparently, Edward just smiled and said, "oh, okay. If there's anything you need this weekend I'll be in Arthur's room."

"So you said earlier, and I'm sure you are going to have some very interesting guy talk all weekend long," I said, laughing. "Good luck with that. I think you might need my help this weekend more than I'll need yours," I said, gently elbowing him. Argh! Quit touching him! He's so totally going to get the wrong idea. "I gotta go feed. Talk to you later." And with that I quickly escaped before anything else could happen.

I busied myself feeding the horses, making sure I was specific about portions and directions from the owners. Most of the riders were in the house having what I assumed was dinner. I figured people would be coming and going all weekend, especially with our haul-ins and the auditors that were planning on coming Saturday and Sunday to watch.

I was also a little nervous. The shadowy figure still lingered in the back of my mind. It could have been just some random incident. But now that we had all these high-class, important people in our barn I was worried he would come back again. Maybe seeing the barn always bustling with activity would deter anyone from coming back. After all, the shadow did come last weekend.

There were a bunch of cars parked in our parking lot with more coming and going. I heard a diesel pulling in which caught my attention because I feared we had miscounted how many horses were actually spending the night. Diesel equals trailer in my happy little world. I walked over to the barn door and realized the truck was not hooked up to a trailer but was still parking with all the other riders' vehicles. I don't remember that truck pulling in earlier. So, being the nosy person I am, I stood in the doorway, not making any effort to hide the fact I was spying.

When I saw who hopped out of the truck I think I gasped but I don't remember. I was so overwhelmed with his presence that my jaw dropped completely to the ground. It was the one and only Sven Pallen, reining gold medal champion in musical freestyle, not only at the Olympics but at two consecutive World Equestrian Games. Holy cow was all that would come to mind.

Sven Pallen was originally from Germany but moved to the United States fifteen years earlier to ride under the U.S. flag. It was a huge move, seeing the German team usually produces some of the best equestrian athletes in the world. He has helped the U.S. team tremendously, bringing his talent, his kindness toward the animals, and his strong work ethic along with him. He was very select about the horses that he chose to ride and the sponsors he accepted. I've always joked around at home that Indie and Sven would be a perfect match for each other, if only I had enough money to sponsor them. Sven, along with most equestrian athletes, did not buy his own horses. The ones he showed were owned by a very wealthy citizen or a large corporation. Showing horses was not a money maker by any stretch of the imagination and therefore there was a need for sponsors to foot the entry fees, the trailering, the stabling, and the grooming and feeding costs. You've got to really love the sport to pursue a professional career or be extremely well off with your finances. Either that or you to be just plain crazy.

Standing in the aisle, drooling, it all started to click. Amy was originally from Germany as well. She did mention that some "friends" were coming that weekend as well as the locals. No wonder she was so picky about who was invited. I quickly got back to work after watching Sven safely make it to the house.

My mind started racing at 100 miles per hour, trying to figure out what was going to happen that weekend. I didn't notice Sven's horse come in unless he was training a different horse. Maybe he was just an auditor. Or perhaps one of his students were riding that weekend and he wanted to show his support. Oh, my brain was starting to hurt and I suddenly felt the pressure I was going to be under that weekend, not just with caring for the horses, but I just remembered I had to ride in front of him!

****

Edward was right. The riders took turns that evening warming up in the arena. Gertrude and I hung out in the viewing room, watching the rides. Some were unproductive in our eyes while others were absolutely amazing to watch. There was a lot of talent there that weekend, and it started to discourage me just a little. If these riders and horses were this good and they were just "local talent" and not on the international circuit what chance did Indie and I have?

I knew it is a far-fetched dream but I also know deep down in my heart that Indie has it. He has what it takes but so do these horses. And here they are. Unknowns. Stuck with the regional circuit, nationally known if they were lucky. I tried not to let that thought dampen my weekend. I still wanted to take notes and hopefully pick up some tips here and there.

"Wow," Gertrude broke into my thoughts. I had filled her in on my Sven encounter earlier in the day and she shared my awe-struck behavior when she saw him in the arena.

He wasn't riding a horse and we came to the conclusion that he was just there to audit and socialize with his fellow teammate. He had just walked in to the arena to join Ms. Arnot in talking with one of the weekend riders. I tried to purposely run into him earlier but I couldn't seem to find him wandering around the barn. Oh well. I'll keep trying.

"Okay, here's the deal," I started, turning toward Gertrude. "If either of us spot him in the barn at all this weekend we are to find each other so we can, um, maybe, um … "

"You want to creep Sven?" Gertrude finally cut in.

"Well, yes, but not in a bad way. No lurking around corners, just keep it casual. I'm determined to talk to him before he leaves this weekend," I said not feeling at all uncomfortable with my proposition.

"What will you say to him?" she asked.

"I don't know. I'm sure something will come out." "Well keep that something appropriate," she warned with a smile.

"Gertrude!" I scolded. "I am the picture of appropriate be-havior," I replied, sticking my nose up in the air to mock my stuck up behavior. She laughed and then quickly stopped.

"Oh no! We're slacking on our creeping already. He's left the arena, along with Amy. Should we try to find him?"

"Let's do it," I said and we both started to stand. Just then the viewing room door opened and in walked Ms. Arnot and Sven, heading right toward us. I felt all the color rushing to my head. Partially because we were in the same room together and partially because I was afraid there was some hidden camera that just heard our plot and now they were on to us.

"Just the two I was looking for," said Ms. Arnot. She seemed, happy? Suddenly I wished Sven could stay with us the rest of the summer just so I could enjoy this different side of Ms. Arnot.

"Sven Pallen, I would like you to meet Gertrude and Dana. Both girls are staying here as working students for the summer." She called me 'girl.' Now I was the happy one.

Sven shook Gertrude's hand first and then mine. He was a tall string bean of a man, about mid-forties, buzz-cut hair, and one of those people that always walked around in his breeches, even if he didn't have a horse to ride. His smile was warm and I could see why he had such a great reputation for his kindness and gentleness in the horse world.

"Gertrude, would you please find Arthur for me. I would like for Sven to meet the last third of your trio," Ms. Arnot asked. Gertrude nodded and quickly hurried off to find Arthur, assuming he hadn't flown the coop for the weekend already. Good luck to her.

After the door closed Ms. Arnot wasted no time at the prime opportunity for the three of us to be alone.

"Dana, I invited Sven here with the sole purpose of watching your Indie. I wanted his opinion and thought that you wouldn't mind his input on your ride. He'll be staying until Wednesday and perhaps we could rearrange your schedules those days if needed."

I'm speechless. No, really, I have no idea what to say. Thank you? Sure? Are you serious? Don't you have more important things to do? Apparently, seeing my brain turmoil Sven stepped in and tried to calm the storm.

"Amy has spoken very highly of you for the past few weeks. I look forward to watching you and your partner this weekend."

"Thanks. I hope we don't disappoint you," was what came out in response. He came here just for me. And Indie, of course.

Holy. Cow.

Thank you, Lord!

Chapter Twelve

"Nice ride, Johanna," Ms. Arnot praised one of the local trainers after her session on Saturday morning. Gertrude and I were trying to sneak peaks in between cleaning stalls and our regular turnouts. So far the morning was going exceptionally well. The riders were all fabulous, friendly, and cooperative when it came to working around our schedule. They were there because they wanted the same thing we wanted: professional help in a highly competitive world.

After all the rides that day there was going to be a catered dinner at the main house for everyone. The three of us had been invited as well and it would be in all our best interest to attend, although I was afraid Arthur had plans to escape as soon as the last horse was taken care of for the evening. Gertrude and I had nothing better to do and were looking forward to rubbing elbows with some of the bigger names in the equine world. Sven was going to be there as well and I assumed everyone would be picking his brain.

We really didn't have time to take showers before dinner so Gertrude and I washed up as best as we could and then headed to the main house for dinner. On the way out of the barn we ran into Edward who, apparently by his delicious woodsman scent, had time to take a shower. Must be nice.

"Things went well today," he stated as if we hadn't noticed.

"Yes, Captain Obvious. We were actually here all day to make sure things ran smoothly," I replied in my classic sarcastic tone. I smirked while Gertrude looked terrified. Edward laughed, noticing how my comment affected poor Gertrude.

"Don't worry," Edward reassured Gertrude. "I've learned to pretty much take everything Dana says as some sort or rhetorical remark aimed at making me feel like less of a man."

I outwardly laughed and realized how loud I was, quickly covering my mouth. Edward joined in the laughter, Gertrude still extremely cautious, only forcing a smile to fit in with what seemed to be an outward show of disobedience. I hooked arms with Gertrude and convinced her it was okay to relax around Edward. The two of them had a weird one-day relationship, one I knew Gertrude regretted deeply. But Edward was an adult and also realized that he had given Gertrude the wrong impression right from the start. I wanted us all to be friends, kind of like we were starting from scratch.

"What is that smell?" Edward questioned, wrinkling his nose as we approached the front door. "It smells like someone forgot to take a shower." He was teasing, of course, but Gertrude was very vain and it took a lot of convincing to even get her to come without a shower. Thankfully, we were all still in a jovial mood but I still hauled off and smacked him in the arm, trying to hide my grin.

"Don't you dare!" I scolded, trying to use my eyes to tell him that it was not cool to joke about such a touchy subject in front of Gertrude. And of course, she started panicking.

"Oh my gosh! Is it me? I knew I should have cleaned up better! What will they think of us, Dana?" Gertrude babbled, half-heartedly turning to walk back to the barn.

"Listen, you are perfectly fine. More beautiful than anyone who just walked out of a barn should be. We are going to go in there, have a good time, and maybe even make some new friends.

Do you understand?" I said, looking right into her eyes. Oh, the damage men do without thinking.

"Okay," was her sheepish reply. I walked past Edward to the door, giving him the ultimate evil eye for the foolishness he had done. He just gave me one of those innocent looks, raising his shoulders as if not knowing what he had done wrong. I wasn't too worried though. I figured staying with Arthur would be torture enough.

Everyone was already started on drinks and appetizers and paid no attention to our arrival. I was glad for that. I didn't want people staring at the dirty barn help that had just seemed to have crashed the party. Gertrude and I hung around together, being each other's buddies in case we needed an excuse to leave if we felt too out of place. Edward had no problem mingling with the crowd. He was quite the people person which was a quality I found very attractive. If only the circumstances were different. In so many ways, I reminded myself of course. The only real thing I knew about Edward was that he cleaned up nicely.

At some point in the evening, after dinner had been consumed, I found myself in a conversation with Sven, Gertrude glued to my side. I didn't picture her as such a wall flower but I assumed because of her self-conscious smell (which had been completely covered up with about a half a bottle of perfume) she was unwilling to part from my side. I was her deflection, in case any of these horse people would dare say anything remotely negative when it came to barn smells. Hello.

I had been patiently waiting since Friday for my ride with Sven. I was looking forward to it and avoiding it all at the same time. I was honored but yet didn't know if I could take the criticism. I knew he was kind and well-loved in the equine world, but my ego could be very fragile when it came to Indie and myself.

We had been a team for six years and everything he knew I've taught him. That could be a downfall if my training wasn't done properly of course.

"I know you have been busy all day but I was wondering if perhaps I could watch you ride tonight." It wasn't really a question, more of a statement that I couldn't refuse.

"Um, sure, I can get him ready now if you'd like."

Now? Was I crazy? I was exhausted and now terrified that I didn't have sufficient mental time to prepare for this very moment.

"Gut," was his smiling reply. It was 'good' in German. "I'll go tell Amy and we'll be out in about, say, thirty minutes?"

"Sure," and I was out the door in a flash, Gertrude on my heels. I was at a full jog as soon as I hit the cobblestone walk way.

"What's going on?" Gertrude asked, running behind me.

"I'm going to get Indie tacked up. Sven wants to see us ride for a little bit I guess." I didn't know what else to tell her because I honestly didn't know myself what was going on.

Gertrude was a huge help to me when we reached the barn and I owed her big time. She got Indie out and started grooming him up for me as I changed into a nice pair of breeches and coordinating top. I felt grubby and hated putting clean clothes on my dirty body but I wanted us to look our best.

I threw on the saddle and bridle and headed to the arena to warm him up and wake him up. Thankfully he was still picking at scraps from his dinner so I knew I wasn't upsetting any nap time. Indie always rode better on a full stomach even though I wasn't too sure if I was going to manage as well as he would.

I had just taken Indie a few times around the arena when Sven and Ms. Arnot showed up.

Okay, Lord. I'm not asking for miracles here, just safety, wisdom, and doggone it, let us shine.

It was easy following Sven's instructions. He was very clear on what he wanted us to do and I tried my best to remember everything I had learned from Ms. Arnot so far in our lessons. After all, they did share many of the basic foundations of teaching dressage.

Sven was kind, and when we didn't do something exactly right he had us try again and again until we both understood what was expected of us. I felt Indie having some major transformation breakthroughs during our lesson. I knew they had been starting earlier with Ms. Arnot but what a difference a day made!

We worked for about an hour before finally cooling out. Sven praised us for a job well-done and for such a nice equine partnership. He was polite and complimentary on our training, but I got the feeling he didn't find what he was after. Oh well. At least I got a great learning opportunity, free of charge.

I noticed a few of the locals had gathered in the viewing room at some point during my ride and were just heading back to the aisleway. No one really spoke to us barn people except for maybe a 'thank you' when they caught us cleaning or feeding their horse. Apparently nothing had changed. I walked past a few of them in the aisle on their way out the door back to the house and no one said anything. Which was fine. I wasn't looking for compliments, but if you were going to take the time to watch my ride I would think a polite 'good ride' was in order. Just saying.

"Good ride," came Gertrude's familiar voice. I smiled at her over my shoulder.

"Thanks! I couldn't have done it without your help tonight. Thank you, thank you, thank you! I totally owe you dinner for this one." Gertrude seemed genuinely happy that she could help and I was happy to see her in such good spirits.

I was seeing a change in Gertrude. She started making an effort to pay more attention to the details in people's rides as well as her own. Yes, she was still constantly connected to her phone and her boyfriend, but she had started to prioritize and I was quite impressed, and pleased.

I put an exhausted Indie back in the tacking stall. Gertrude helped me groom him and then finished putting away the rest of my tack, jabbering on about so and so and how their ride went that day and how their ride was going to go tomorrow if they actually did what Amy told them to do.

I've learned how to hear the words coming out of Gertrude's mouth but not really have to listen to her stories. As long as I am there to talk to, throwing in a few nods, ohhs, and ahhs, she seems content. Only when she seems truly distressed do I actually turn on my listening ears. I do like her and want to help her if I can with the important stuff, like her love life and how to follow the barn schedule.

"So do you think there's anything going on between Amy and Sven?" she asked in a hushed voice. It caught me by surprise, the quick change in topic and I had to take a moment to let what she just said stick in my brain.

"Um, I guess I haven't really put much thought into the possibility. He is her teammate so I can see that they would be close. But he is all the way in California. Don't you think something more might have happened by now if there was something?"

Oh great. I'm getting sucked into her little world of trying to figure out people's lives that I have no business trying to figure out.

"Well, I think they'd make a cute couple. Both with those accents, and being such accomplished horse people. I think it would be a perfect match," she smiled with delight. "Kind of like you and Edward."

"Gertrude!" I scolded. I'd done a lot of scolding that day and it wasn't becoming whatsoever. She just looked at me, all innocent, but I saw her devilish grin just waiting to appear.

I gave her the evil eye, knowing that she was just trying to get me going. My feelings toward Edward were that of the mixed variety and I really wasn't going to discuss that with her. Plus, there really wasn't anything to discuss. I preferred to date people who actually lived within my same country. Period. It was a bonus that he had experience with horses and a mutual respect for the sport .... What am I saying? There's nothing there but a great friendship.

"Oh, come on, Dana. You know he's super hot. And the way he looks at you is something that every girl would love to have."

God bless Gertrude. She certainly knows how to make a girl feel good about herself. It was like her one-day fling with Edward never happened. I'm not sure why she was so adamant about pushing me on Edward but I just tried to let it roll off my back.

"Thanks, Gertrude. But really, Edward and I are just friends and that is how it's going to stay."

"But I just want to see you happy," she almost whined. Ah-ha! There it was. She thought I wasn't happy because I didn't have someone. I had to search for the right words because here was my opportunity.

"But I am happy, Gert. I find my joy with the horses and I always have God to talk to when I am lonely, scared, happy, sad, well, anytime. He's always there for me and has given me such peace in any circumstance. If He wants me to be with someone it will happen. Until then, I'm content." Wow, that actually made sense to me. And it is the truth. I am content. Yes, every one of my friends is married and most of them have started their own families but that isn't the plan for my life right now.

I've been given bigger and better plans. Being here, for example. This never would have been able to happen had my circumstances been different. I've been waiting patiently for something like this to happen and the door finally opened. And let me tell you, I leapt through that sucker without looking back.

It was an answer to prayer being able to expand my skills and venture out of my comfort zone back home. Indie and I have overcome some pretty big obstacles in our lifetime together, ones in which I didn't think we would make it through. There was even a point when Indie was injured that a vet told me he was no good and to just put him down. God certainly works in mysterious ways.

I could tell Gertrude didn't quite understand what I was saying, but I felt good that I was able to share with her what makes me so strong.

"I admire you, Dana. You are such a good, kind, and helping person. I don't always understand why you do what you do but I respect that about you. And to think, all this time I didn't really think Amy even liked you. At all."

Yeah, me either.

"You are just as strong, Gertrude. Just have more faith in yourself and don't let others tell you what to do. Well, you'll have to do what Ms. Arnot tells you but I'm looking more at the big picture here," I felt the need to clarify. "If training is what you want to do, then do it. If there feels like there is something else that you would like to try, then do it. But you have to try and not give up just because something becomes difficult, or maybe someone has a better horse than you. We all can't be Olympic riders even though that's what we all want." Speaking more for myself right now. I hope I'm helping and not making her more confused.

During our talk we had absentmindedly put everything away and cleaned up all my mess. I looked around, noticing everything was done. Gertrude looked around too. We both laughed, realizing how second nature this whole horse thing was to both of us.

"I'm going to give Indie his treats. Why don't you go back and get washed up. I'll be there in a minute. I'm actually kind of hungry, too." I think all my nerves had finally settled and now my stomach needed more fuel.

"Sounds like a plan! I'll pop some popcorn," she replied as she headed back to our room. Once I heard our door shut I got a creepy feeling. Everyone had gone back up to the house already and Arthur was gone for the night, or weekend, depending on how he feels. I started humming to myself, a habit I started back at my barn when I did night checks. For some reason it made me feel safer humming a tune out loud, just in case I needed to scare away any coyotes or wild deer. Our deer can get awful aggressive.

I had a bucket full of treats in my hand as I headed toward Indie's stall, still humming "Our God is an Awesome God" when I heard someone join in my chorus.

Easily frightened, I literally threw the can of treats up in the air and half-jumped, half-ran to Indie's stall. Was I really expecting my horse to protect me when I got there? I mean, I know my horse is big and all but he is deathly afraid of cats, and now probably me and my hyperactive behavior.

"So sorry, I should have known you frighten easily," came a man's voice. It took a moment to register who it belonged to seeing that my overactive imagination was already in full gear.

"What are you doing creeping around the barn?" I demanded, not letting myself fully relax. It was weird seeing Edward at the barn at that time of night. I had totally forgotten that he was staying in Arthur's room that weekend.

A deep, genuine laugh came from him as he slowly approached me, still plastered to Indie's stall. He was being cautious, as well he should be after what just happened.

"I'm not creeping. I'm checking on all the horses. I figured after your ride you would be too tired, so I thought I'd do it for you, just for tonight of course," his eyes smiled. Oh, those eyes. Even in the darkened barn they were delightfully enchanting.

"Well, thank you, I think. But trust me, I'm fully awake now no thanks to you." I wasn't mad at him but actually thankful for the fact that it was him and not one of the weekend riders. Or the shadow. Edward was bent down on the floor, picking up all the treats that I had so carelessly thrown just a few moments earlier.

"Well, the least I can do is help clean up this mess I made for you," he said, looking up at me from the aisle floor, that boyish grin still lingering on his scruffy face. Wow. In order to not feel so uncomfortable with the position I quickly bent down and helped as well.

We finished cleaning up the treats and I dumped them in Indie's bucket. He was happy and now totally oblivious to what just happened to him two minutes ago. Oh, to be a horse and just live in the moment. Life could be so much easier for us if we could do the same.

"I heard what you said to Gertrude earlier," he started as he petted Indie's forehead through the bars. First of all, Indie would never in a million years let me do that to him while he was eating. Traitor.

"Oh, what part was that?" I asked, racking my brain trying to rethink the conversation I just had with my roommate. I was only getting bits and pieces and I knew they weren't in the right order in my head. Curse that concussion and the short-term memory loss.

"About why you do all this," he said, gesturing with his hands at the barn and the horses. "I haven't been around horses to the extent that you have but you truly have a passion for the sport that I haven't seen in a lot of people. I'm sure Gertrude is not the only person who has ever looked up to you." He paused. I didn't like the pause. Someone needed to fill the empty air because I wasn't comfortable with all these accolades, let alone have them all happen in one day.

"Thank you. But I do all this," I said, copying his gesture, "because I've been given the opportunity and I love it. Plain and simple." I kept my gaze on Indie to keep from being lured into his kindness.

"Ah, but there is nothing plain and simple about you, Miss Dana." Out of my peripheral vision I could see, and feel him getting closer. Time to call it a night.

But I couldn't. I felt trapped, but not necessarily in a bad way. Our eyes met as he raised his hand, obviously not to gently brush away a stray strand of hair since mine was all neatly tucked under my do-rag. Instead, he rested it carefully on shoulder and spoke quietly.

"You really believe God has a plan for you?" he asked. He wasn't asking in a way that made me question God or get defensive, but in a way that made me more confident and reassured in my faith.

"Yes," was my just as quiet reply. I felt the heat rushing to my face, not knowing what he was going for here.

"Are you ready for what He has in store?"

"Yes."

"Then you best be ready to hold on to your breeches. You have quite the ride ahead of you," he said in earnest.

Chapter Thirteen

All night long I replayed Edward's words over and over again, not wanting to forget them or misunderstand them. The other thought that kept playing in my mind was that fact that Edward seemed to have a pretty strong faith as well. It didn't dawn on me until later that he was singing a Christian song when he snuck up on me that night. I certainly had some questions for him. All this time trying to avoid him when I should have taken advantage of this potential brother in Christ.

I tried counting sheep. I even tried quietly exercising to put my mind to rest, but nothing was helping. I'm glad tomorrow is Sunday. If I'm at all lucky I can sneak in a little nap in the afternoon during one of the rides. I really hated the thought of not taking advantage of all the teaching going on but I also know how unpleasant I am if I don't get enough sleep.

If only I could turn on a small lamp and read. Reading always puts me to sleep, but I didn't want to wake Gertrude. We had a bit of a conversation before bed after I told her I ran into Edward in the aisle doing night checks. She poked and prodded but I gave nothing away about my conversation with him. She was just looking for mushy details anyway and I didn't have any of those to give her.

I also purposely neglected to tell her about my almost close encounter with a more physical Edward. I kept that bazaar memory to myself. Although nothing happened I feel strangely closer to Edward and I started thinking of all the things I needed to ask him tomorrow, such as what in the world was he talking about.

Tossing and turning I decided that my bedtime prayer was not enough. I went into an all out conversation with God in hopes of easing my mind from the confusing yet wonderful day. I told myself not to look at the clock but my eyes had stolen a glance at 1:30 a.m. as I flipped myself over on my stomach. I slept better in that position even though my back would pay for it in the morning. Before I knew it the alarm was going off and I was startled awake.

Awake was a good sign. It meant I had finally fallen asleep at some point the night before. I was not sure where my conversation with God ended but He had been merciful enough to slip me into a deep sleep. I slithered out of bed and talked myself into the fact that I had a lot to accomplish that day and I had no time to waste.

I changed into my dirty barn clothes as Gertrude set out the bowls for breakfast. I was very thankful for my roommate. She may drive me nuts in her lack of common sense but it was nice to have someone around who was kind and caring.

After breakfast we both went our separate ways, me to feeding and Gertrude to start turning out and cleaning stalls. I desperately missed going to church on Sundays and I didn't have the nerve to ask Ms. Arnot for the time off in the morning to attend a service. Plus, we were in Canada. Did they have the same denominations as us Americans? I decided to be content with my Bible and devotional book that my sister had packed for me before I left.

The riders started making their way to the barn around eight o'clock in the morning, just in time to start preparing for their nine o'clock rides. By nine I was starting to get tired and was thankful that Indie had a good workout the day before. If I don't ride or turn him out today I won't worry. He would probably enjoy the day off.

I figured watching a ride might help initiate some REM patterns so I made my way to the viewing room to sit with a few of the other riders who were socializing as they waited for their turn. I found Edward at the coffee pot, counting out just the right amount of grounds to make a fresh brew. It wasn't the perfect setting but it would have to do.

"Hey," I said as I walked up next to him at the table.

"Hey," he smiled back. I was temporarily frozen by his gaze but then shook it off and remembered why I had approached him in the first place.

"Question," I started but then I didn't know how to ask without sounding tacky. "Um, I don't really know how to ask, and honestly I don't really know if it's a question or not … last night…." I paused, looking to him in hopes that he would catch my drift and answer my unasked questions.

He didn't. He just stood their and smiled. It was one of those comforting smiles, not the kind that say 'I have a secret and won't tell you' kind of smiles.

"While you are trying to figure out your question in that beautiful mind of yours I have one for you," he started. "Do you always hum when you're nervous?"

Finally, an opening.

"Good question. But I have one in return. Do you only join in to the humming when you know the song?"

"Ha!" he laughed aloud. "Rich Mullins and I go way back."

"I'm curious to know how you and Rich know each other so well," I said, keeping my voice quiet seeing that the ride had already started.

"I'll fill you in later," he replied just as softly, eyes dancing. "Anything else?" he asked as he turned to rest his backside on the coffee table.

"Yes, actually," I started. I looked around to see if anyone was listening in on our conversation and then looked back at Edward, feeling more comfortable with being in his presence. "What did you mean about being ready? Is there something I should know?"

His pause and the somewhat twisted look in his once relaxed smile led me to believe that there was something more to our conversation the night before. I waited, patiently for once.

"Dana, may I see you for a moment?" came Sven's voice from behind me. I didn't even realize he had come into the lounge.

"Certainly," I answered cheerfully. Sven turned to walk back out into the aisle and I quickly realized I was supposed to follow. I started walking when I felt Edward gently grab my arm. I turned to see his soft, kind smile return to his face. He didn't say anything at all but I felt strength and security as he slowly let go, throwing his look to the door as if to indicate I best get moving.

Why was everything feeling so weird? It was as if Edward was a totally different person even though he hadn't changed a bit. I changed my perception of him the night before and I felt sad for judging him so quickly when we met at the farm. And here I thought I was doing so good.

Clearing my head I quickly caught up with Sven out in the aisle near Indie's stall. What could he possibly want now?

"I wanted to ask your permission to ride Indie later on this afternoon," he asked ever so politely. I was so excited that I practically jumped and said yes at the same time. He smiled and said he would be back around four o'clock to ride. I wondered if weird was the new lifestyle I was going to have to adopt after all was said and done here in Canada. So far, I'm okay with the idea.

I spent the next few hours wiping down my tack and getting Indie prepared for his big ride. It was only one o'clock and I was finally winding down, again, from all the morning excitement. I thought I would squeeze in a twenty-minute nap before finishing up for the afternoon. I opened the door to our room only to find Gertrude entertaining some of the riders who had already ridden. They were watching footage from the previous year's FEI games and I really didn't feel like joining them.

I said a quick hello and then left with my alarm clock, wondering if I could sneak in one of the trailers and catch a nap. And then I had an idea. A really bad idea, but I was desperate.

I hurried over to the other side of the barn and knocked on Arthur's door. No one answered. Oh well, it was worth a shot. I had just started walking away when I heard the toilet flush in the bathroom right next door. Not wanting to be caught hanging around the bathroom I scooted away as quickly as I could down the barn aisle in the opposite direction.

Once I heard the door open I turned back to see who it was and was glad to see it was Edward. I turned around and headed back toward him.

"Were you looking for me?" he asked, hope in his voice.

"Yes, well, no. I was technically looking for Arthur but I should have known he wouldn't be back yet," I started blabbering. "Any-who, I have a huge favor to ask. Do you mind if I borrow your room for about twenty minutes? I'm totally exhausted and just need a few minutes to rest my eyes before this afternoon. Can you spare me a rental?" I asked, hoping he wouldn't find it as awkward as I found my current situation.

"Sure, come on in. But be forewarned. This is *not* my place of residence so I am not held accountable for anything odd or disturbing that you may see when you enter." He was joking, I was sure. But at that point I really didn't plan on inspecting the place, just sleeping in it.

I was pleasantly surprised that there was no dirty-person smell or foul odors coming from inside the room. It actually smelled really good. Like Edward.

Great. Was I really going to get any sleep here, constantly whiffing the woodsman scent that defined Edward? Warm, welcoming, like a real man. He pointed to his bed and I shook my head.

"I'll take Arthur's," I replied to his invitation. I looked over to Arthur's bed and quickly changed my mind. "On second thought, I'll take yours."

I tossed off my shoes and laid down before Edward was even out the door.

"Hey," I called out quietly. "Thanks."

"Anytime I can help," he replied with that smile and those dancing eyes. And with that he was gone, and so was I.

****

Twenty minutes later my alarm went off and I hit the snooze. I usually never hit the snooze but it was such a peaceful sleep I really didn't want it to end. I laid there realizing that all good things come to an end and I reminded myself to thank God for the past weekend. So many things had come out of the weekend, and to top it all off ,they were all good things. I rolled over to get out of bed and was startled to see Edward at the kitchen table.

"How long have you been here?" I asked, feeling suddenly like an imposition.

"Hours, waiting for you to get out of my bed, Goldilocks." He was sipping something and reading a magazine. He was also chuckling to himself. I didn't find it funny because I panicked, thinking I had set my alarm wrong. Seeing the terror in my face he quickly corrected his earlier comment. "I just stepped in about two minutes ago. I know you only said twenty minutes so I wanted to make sure you were up in time, just in case your alarm didn't go off."

Well if that wasn't the sweetest thing anyone has ever done for me. Wrap this guy up and send him to Ohio. I could certainly use him there.

"Thanks," I said, almost sheepishly. "I better get going. But first, do you know why Sven is here?" I had to know if there was some ulterior motive to his mini-vacation here at the farm.

"I know my aunt and him are very close friends. Perhaps it was just a nice weekend get-away with old friends." I noticed he kept his nose in his magazine while he talked.

"Um, okay. Sounds possible, but I don't think that's it." I was trying to get some reaction out of him but he maintained his reading pose.

I stood up and walked over to the table, pulled out a chair, and sat down right across from him. I stared. He wouldn't look up. I poked him in the arm with my finger. He still didn't look up, but I did get a smirk that he was desperately trying to hold in.

"So how many times have you just read that same sentence right there in your article?" I asked, pointing at his magazine.

"Enough to still not know what it says so you best get going so I can concentrate," he replied, smiling but eyes still glued to the page.

"Hey, so any more with our shadowy friend?" I asked, trying to get his attention from a different angle.

"Nope. Must have been just a passer-by," was his steady reply.

Okay, enough was enough. I grabbed the magazine and quickly threw it behind my back, holding it prisoner between my back and the chair until I could get some answers. I finally had his attention and his surprised eyes met mine.

"I can't believe you just stole my magazine!" he exclaimed, laughing.

"I can't believe you won't help me out here! I feel I've been left in the dark with something that might pertain to me," I said, slightly raising my voice. Not because I was mad, but because I had started a friendly war that I wasn't really intending to start. And I started fearing the retaliation from Edward.

He slowly leaned forward across the table, arms sliding out in front of him as if he was planning on stretching his arms long enough to reach around the back of my chair. The closer he got the more I feared he might actually be able to reach.

"Hey," I said as sternly as I could muster. "You give me some answers and I'll give you your magazine."

"Ah, but this is more fun, watching you squirm." I held my ground, even when he stood up and with one step was around the side of the table standing right next to me. He bent down toward me, one hand resting on the table and one on the back of my chair. Did the heat just kick on? I could literally feel his breath on my face. And then before I knew it his handsome face broke into the most amazing smile and he walked away, magazine in hand.

Chapter Fourteen

It was four o'clock. Indie was all tacked up and being mounted by Sven. I had my video camera ready to go even though I was shaking, worried again that Indie might do something to harm the rider. I prayed he would be a good boy and deep down I knew that all would go well. Indie loved men riders.

Some of the other riders had already headed home, but some still stuck around and watched from the viewing room. I watched from the inside of the arena, Gertrude standing by my side for support. She started off watching with me and then apparently got bored and went back to the barn to work on some more stalls after a few minutes.

About halfway through the ride I felt a hand on my lower back, but I was watching Sven work on three tempis across the arena and I didn't want to miss any of them on film. The hand lingered and I caught a whiff of that wonderful woodsman smell. Keeping the camera running I turned my head to acknowledge Edward with a smile. He was already smiling. I was thankful when his hand finally pulled away from my back.

Sven had taken a walk break with Indie and I decided to swing the camera in Edward's direction before turning it off. I figured a quick glimpse would be all I would have to remember him by after I went home.

"Wave to my peeps in Ohio!" I whispered. Edward, the trooper that he is, grinned and waved at the camera. We quietly laughed together and then turned the camera off.

"Looking good," he said as he looked at me. "The horse, of course." A smile and a wink followed. I just rolled my eyes and turned my attention back to Indie. Sven was riding toward me and although he had not yet been on Indie for more than 35 minutes he apparently was done. I tried to hide my disappointment but walked over with a smile plastered on my face.

"Thank you, Mr. Pallen. That was a wonderful ride," I said, hoping that Sven wouldn't have the heart to deflate my perception of the ride.

"You're most welcome. Thank you for allowing me to ride," was his smiling reply. He was known for his kindness so I knew he wouldn't add on any additional negative comments. Only constructive criticism. But even that never came. He just simply handed me my horse and walked back up to the house with Ms. Arnot.

Apparently I was unable to hide my disappointment from Edward. He moved closer and gently laid a hand on my shoulder.

"Just think. Now you have evidence that *two* world-class equestrians rode your horse. Gertrude and Arthur can't say that." He was trying to help and I appreciated that. But it wasn't a competition to see whose horse could be ridden by the most people. Then again, I'm not sure what it really was anymore. People just enjoyed riding Indie I guess. I should be happy that he hasn't bucked anyone off, yet.

Edward walked back to the barn with me and Indie and unwrapped his polo wraps while I took off the saddle and bridle. We worked in comfortable silence for a while until we heard gravel crunching. My guess: Arthur was back.

"Sounds like your roomy is back."

"That's okay. I'm actually moving all my stuff back up to the house tonight. I'm kind of glad I didn't have to share the space with Arthur. That dude is a little weird."

My jaw dropped slightly and I quickly gave him the quiet sign. Who knows who was still roaming around the barn. Edward looked around with shifty eyes, as if mocking me and my concern. He picked up Indie's four wraps and walked over to where I was standing, brushing Indie. Without asking where they went he threw them around my neck, all the sweat and arena sand scratching at my neck.

"Eww!" I hollered. "That is so gross!" I grabbed all four wraps and quickly threw them on the ground.

Edward walked away, laughing. He stopped by Indie's head to give him a couple good scratches. "It's not like you're clean or anything. You kind of stink like a horse. Besides, you'll have time to take a shower before dinner tonight."

"What do you mean?"

"Oh, I must have forgotten to give you the message. Perhaps it was when you were snoring away on my bed." I wasn't going to live that one down. "Amy invited the three of you to dinner at the house tonight. I think it's to wrap up what went on this weekend. I do believe there are two guests who aren't leaving until tomorrow morning so they will be joining us as well. Better wash up this time." With a wink he disappeared down the aisle.

I went back to grooming my horse and started to think of how quickly things had changed. I went from trying to avoid Edward, his charm and good looks, to becoming what seemed like old pals. It was totally comfortable being around him and I wondered if it was because I found out he had some kind of a Christian background. I still was unsure of the complete history but I also knew I would be able to ask him. It was a nice change and, like most other times, I regretted that it didn't happen sooner.

There were still so many things that I questioned here on the farm. Not to mention the fact that people seemed really good at keeping secrets. Perhaps having shadowy strangers running in and out of your barn is not unusual up here. Call me crazy but as a barn owner I would be making sure I was taking every precaution so it would not happen again. I still felt it was my duty to keep a close eye on things, even during the week when I wasn't technically in charge anymore.

****

Gertrude, Arthur, and I walked up to the main house about an hour later. Thankfully Arthur was sober. He was also bummed to find out a handsome man had been using his room all weekend and that he missed out.

I made a special effort to look nice that night. I didn't really bring any dressy clothes on the trip but I did my best to look presentable. Sven had never really seen me in anything but my barn clothes. I didn't want him to start thinking I was just someone's barn help for the summer. This was my chance to represent Indie and myself as well-deserving members of the United States Dressage Federation.

I rang the bell even though Arthur insisted we walk right in. I kindly reminded him we were guests, not permanent residents. Edward seemed to have been waiting at the door because it opened almost as instantly as I rang the bell.

You could smell the wonderful aromas of dinner, homemade obviously, coming from the open door along with the delicious scent of Edward. Easy girl, I reminded myself. Arthur and Gertrude shuffled past me seeing that I was just standing there blocking the doorway, staring at a dashingly handsome, clean-shaven

Edward. His gaze seemed to be fixed as well. If only ....

"See, you had plenty of time to clean up nicely," he said.

"Thanks. You're not so bad yourself," I smiled back. Funny how a clean pair of jeans and a nice tee will make a world of difference. I stepped through the door and made my way to the dining room, where everyone else was already congregating. I walked to the kitchen to see if Ms. Arnot needed any help bringing things out to the table.

"That would be wonderful. Please bring those two dishes and set them in the middle of the table," was her response.

Goodness. The dishes even had designated places. Apparently Ms. Arnot not only treated her students with strict discipline. She expected it from her dinnerware as well.

I walked the dishes in and set them down where instructed. Everyone had apparently already claimed a seat, including Arthur and Gertrude. There were two vacant spots. One at the head of the table, obviously for our host, and then one next to Edward. I wondered if that was planned by Gertrude or Edward. Or both.

I walked back into the kitchen to see if there was anything else I could help with before having to spend the next forty minutes sitting next to Edward. Ms. Arnot was just bringing out the last dish and encouraged me to sit and relax.

There was constant chatter happening at the table. Sometimes one conversation was taking place, sometimes several at once. There were a total of eight of us at the table and supper seemed to be breezing by nicely. It was strangely nice eating next to Edward, but I was glad not to be directly across from him. I'm well-known for my ability to get food stuck in my teeth and it can get very embarrassing.

Halfway through dinner, Edward asked to excuse himself after sneaking a peek at his cell phone. I never heard it go off but perhaps he had it on vibrate. That was polite. He was gone for all of ten minutes before returning to the table. I smiled in his direction and he returned it with one of his own. I took a minute to study his face, a bit flushed but not tense. I wonder what the phone conversation was about.

None of my business, I reminded myself.

As we were all finishing up with the main course Ms. Arnot starting rising from her chair and clinking her glass to get everyone's attention. We all obediently quieted down and gave her our full attention. She looked very lovely that night in a light tie-at-the-waist blouse, Capri pants, and tall brown boots. I never imagined I would have had to bring dress-up clothes but I was totally comfy in my jeans and tee.

Gertrude, on the other hand, always seemed prepared for anything. She too was dressed up, wearing a shear white tank top, extremely short and extremely tight black shorts, and, get this, high heels. She offered me one of her outfits but after seeing her that evening back in our room I politely declined. There was no way all of me would fit into one of those outfits.

"First, I would like to thank everyone's hard work this weekend. Things went very nicely and I am certain all of our riders enjoyed their stay." She made this comment directed toward the three remaining riders sitting at the table. "Also, thanks to Sven for coming all the way from California to scope out the talent that was here this weekend."

We all raised our glasses along with her, toasting to a successful weekend. After the toast, dessert was brought out and consumed over the same chit-chat that had taken place earlier. I was glad that we didn't have to eat in the house for every meal. It felt a bit stuffy and I wasn't really a part of any conversation. I just mostly listened and nodded.

After dessert I excused myself to go back to the barn and check on the horses. I said goodnight to everyone and again thanked Ms. Arnot for inviting us all over for such a wonderful dinner. Gertrude followed my lead but Arthur chose to stay and continue to catch up on everything he had missed in his absence.

****

Monday morning was pretty much back to normal except that the final three horses would be leaving right after breakfast. After feeding I went back to my regular routine of cleaning the stalls, turning out the horses, and getting them ready for riding. With Anabella out of town we had a little extra work riding but I was okay with that. Ms. Arnot seemed to trust our riding abilities and allowed us to work her show horses. Rinaldi was still only brought out for us for special occasions.

I had happened to walk down the other aisle to drop off an empty wheelbarrow for Arthur and heard men's voices. Being the nosy person I am I quietly made my way over toward the office. Two men were having a conversation and by the thick German accent I knew one of those men were Sven. The other was Edward. The door was slightly ajar so I mingled around the door, keeping an eye out for anyone coming down the aisle. I tried to make out their conversation but I was only getting bits and pieces.

"That is a very generous offer, Mr. Pallen. I will definitely look into it and see what I can do," was Edward's reply to an earlier comment made by Sven. His tone held a hint of surprise and I was dying to know what was so generous of Sven.

"Please do consider," Sven responded. "I think this would be a step in the right direction for both farms involved."

"Whatcha doin'?" came Arthur's sly, high-pitched little voice from directly behind me. Of course I jumped and gasped, then realizing the men could probably hear me I quickly walked away, hoping Arthur wouldn't follow me.

He did.

"Did you hear anything good?" he asked in all curiousness. "I've been trying for the past ten minutes to listen in but I just kept getting distracted." He looked eager to learn what I had heard and I decided right then and there that I hadn't heard anything.

"Well, I could have heard more if you hadn't come up and scared me!" I replied, sounding a bit disgruntled. "I've got to get back to work. If you want to know what they are saying then you can go and listen in," was my reply before heading back around the corner to the other side of the barn.

I didn't think too hard on the subject for the simple reason that I didn't have all the facts. But what did Sven mean that it would be a step in the right direction for both farms involved? This farm? His farm? Apparently there was another reason for Sven's little trip to Canada.

I was in one of my stalls currently unoccupied by a horse cleaning and thinking about what I had overheard when I heard the men's voices again. I continued cleaning but kept myself as quiet as a church mouse. It's not like they didn't know we were all in the barn somewhere so it must not be that private of a conversation. Gertrude was out riding one of the horses so I didn't have to worry about her ruining my cover.

There was a bunch of jibber jabber but then I heard a distinct "thank you again" from Edward. I peeked my head out just in time to see the two men, standing in the front doorway, shaking hands. Sven walked out, apparently heading toward the house and Edward just stood there, watching after him. He seemed awfully pensive as he gazed out the front door.

Without warning Edward turned to walk back into the barn and just happened to catch my peeking head leaning halfway out of the horse's stall. I quickly ducked back into the stall and started feverishly cleaning. I feared it was too late, my mind racing to think of an excuse or just something to say when he confronted me.

"Hey," he said, stopping to peer between the bars as if looking at a wild horse.

"Hey," was my nonchalant reply. I kept cleaning while he kept standing there as if he were waiting for something to come out of his mouth. I stopped cleaning for a moment.

"Everything okay?" I asked finally. He thought for a while and then answered.

"Yeah, I guess. I," he paused. I could see his brain searching for the right words but I had a feeling they weren't going to come out. "I've got some work to catch up on in the office. See you around," he finished, still standing there and searching my eyes for some kind of confirmation.

"Okay," was all I could say but then quickly added, "if you need to talk, let me know. I'm here for you."

Did I really mean that?

Edward's eyes lit up ever so slightly.

I guess I really did.

Chapter Fifteen

I was just putting away my dish from dinner when I heard a knock on the door. Gertrude was the closest so she walked over to see who was visiting at the odd hour. All the horses had been fed, turned out, and even ridden. The only thing left to do was night checks later on that evening.

"Hi, Amy. Come on in," I heard Gertrude saying after opening the door. I was thankful that Gertrude and I were neat people. Ms. Arnot doesn't really bother us when our official duties are done for the day even though I knew she expected us to be on watch 24/7 since we were on the property. That was fine. I didn't mind keeping an ear out for strange noises. I had still been on high alert since the shadow incident, but because nothing had happened since then I had become more relaxed.

"Thank you, Gertrude. I am actually here to speak with Dana." I finished what I was doing and walked toward her, not sure what to expect.

"Certainly. What can I do for you?" I asked.

"Would you mind following me to my office." It actually wasn't a question, more like a command. I quickly agreed and followed her out the door. We walked in silence to her office, and the whole time I was thinking to myself that I should be used to these little impromptu meetings with Ms. Arnot. But they still made me nervous as all get out.

I closed the door behind me once we were both inside and realized Sven was in there already, apparently waiting for us.

I made myself as comfortable as I could when she commanded that I 'sit.' She was still gruff but I felt that she still liked me deep down. I wasn't trying to be her friend, nor did I want that responsibility. But I did want her to respect me as a rider and not just some ordinary person who decided to spend the summer away from home.

"I'll get to the point."

Great. Make it quick and painless.

"Sven and I have been talking and we feel that we have both come to the same conclusion." She nodded over to Sven, obviously to turn my attention to him.

"I have a program that I run at my farm in California. It is for elite riders that I have personally hand-selected to ride under my tutelage. After watching your rides and experiencing your horse for myself I feel you would be an asset to my program."

I'm sorry, what is happening here? I feel like what I'm hearing and what my mind is processing can't possibly be the same things. I could feel the blank expression on my face and willed it to become something different.

"Um," was all I could muster. After another brief moment that felt like eternity I tried again. "That sounds wonderful! But are you sure you want both of us?"

Sven laughed and replied, "Of course! Currently, I have four other students who are working with me, two which qualified for the Pan Am games. Maybe I should first ask you what your goals are with Indie."

"Goals, right. Well I guess I could sound cliché and say just like any other athlete I would love to ride internationally. I know Indie has some weaknesses but the potential is inside of him. I don't want his skills and talents to be wasted."

"Well then it sounds like a perfect match," Ms. Arnot chimed in. Why was she pushing this on me? I mean, I'm glad that she is but it just all seems too unreal right now.

"How long would we be with you? I mean, I do have a regular job that pays the bills."

Sven and Ms. Arnot both looked at each other with the faintest of smiles hinting on their faces.

"Dana, if you would accept this opportunity then all your expenses will be paid for by your sponsors and donors. With the bloodlines your horse possesses you will have plenty of willing participants to donate their funds. As for time, you would be with me until you felt you no longer needed my assistance. Three of my students have been with me now for seven years."

I think my jaw just dropped. Seven years? In California? Away from my family? I don't know if I can do that. But what an opportunity. What a dilemma.

"I know this is a big decision and I respect your time thinking it over. I'm not leaving until Wednesday so you have some time to ask more questions should you think of any," Sven offered, his kindness willing me to jump out of my chair and scream 'YES!' But I refrained. It was a lot to think about and I would definitely need to talk all of it over with my family. I already knew what they would say but it was ultimately my decision.

"Thank you so much for the offer and I will definitely think it over." I rose to shake his hand and then headed for the door. I was hoping the conversation was over because all I wanted to do was get out of there and breathe. My knees felt weak and my heart refused to slow down. I just wanted to explode with joy and excitement but I didn't know who I could explode to. If I talked to Gertrude it might seem that I was rubbing it in and Arthur was definitely out of the question. Although I would love to see the expression on his face ....

I paced up and down the aisle, not really wanting to go back to the room but not knowing where else to go to think. I heard the tractor outside and remembered the few trails in the back where I could be in peace. I headed out the door and started praying as soon as my feet hit the gravel. I would have started running but it was still quite muggy and hot.

Please, Lord, give me wisdom in making the right choice. Not only for me and Indie but for You as well. This is bigger than me and I need Your help in choosing the right path and learning to be the light for You.

I continued to walk hoping that God would just shout down an answer, but I knew that wasn't going to happen. God must find humor in the people He created without patience. Unfortunately, I didn't find it very humorous. I sat down on a stump and bowed my head.

My prayer seemed to be the same thing over and over for the past ten minutes but I didn't know what else to ask for. I started to get deep in the thought of what it would actually mean for me. A total lifestyle change. Nothing would ever be the same and I remembered how well I handle change. Not very well.

I would be leaving my family behind. My wonderful supportive parents who gave everything to allow us to live out our equestrian dreams. My all-wise and knowing sister who was always there when I made mistakes or needed a push. What would I do without them?

But now was the time. I had no family of my own, no attachments to any particular people outside my immediate family unit. So it would only make sense taking the next step in my horse career. I felt the tears working their way to the edges of my eyelids.

Deep in thought I did not notice that it was starting to get dark until I heard a noise and looked up. I panicked just for a moment realizing I needed to get going back to the barn but continued to hear the noise getting closer. Great. Just what I needed. Confrontation with a deer tonight. I really despised deer and their secret ambition to attack us humans.

"What are you doing?" I heard Edward ask. I let out a giant sigh, not even realizing I had been holding my breath. I felt exhausted and quickly wiped my eyes to erase any incriminating residue of my tears.

"Oh, just came out here to be one with nature. You know how that goes." I tried to make light of the situation.

"Really? Looked to me like you were quite deep in thought. Anything I can help you with?"

I thought about it. Edward would be the only one who would not feel insulted, irritated, or angry at my predicament. So I decided to keep it as simple as possible.

"Sven and Ms. Arnot talked to me this evening and offered me a great opportunity that I don't know what to do with," was my response.

"Oh?" Edward looked genuinely surprised. "And you're having a difficult time deciding what is the right thing to do?"

"Yeah, but I just spent the last, well, who knows how long I've been out here, throwing it all up to God so I'm hoping I'll get my answer, soon."

"It must be in the air," he said. "Come on, let's get heading back to the barn before the coyotes get us," he said as he extended his hand toward me. I looked at it before slowly reaching out and taking his support. It was like holding hands with your best friend, full of comfort and strength and warmth. Weird. I've never had this feeling before.

We walked a few feet before I realized what he had said earlier. "What did you mean 'it must be in the air'?"

"Oh, I've got my own decisions to make. But I don't know if

my faith is as strong as yours. I've asked for help in the past but I've never really heard an answer. Ever." He seemed more disappointed than mad or angry.

"Sometimes you can't hear Him but you can see Him working. Look at me for example. This trip didn't just happen because He told me to go. I had several doors open along the way to make this possible because I believed."

We continued our way out of the woods in silence. I didn't want to let go of the physical connection we had but I knew it was time. I gently slid my hand out of his strong but soft grasp as we got closer to the barn. He casually put his hand back into his pocket and continued walking by my side as if all of it was second nature. It shouldn't be but it felt that way to me as well.

As we approached the barn door Edward slowed to a stop. I stopped as well wondering how that night was going to end. I still had night checks to do and Edward was no longer living in the barn so there was no legitimate excuse for him to follow me.

"You let me know how that decision-making goes," he smiled down at me.

"And you do the same. Don't give up on hearing God. Just start opening your eyes and see what He's already given you." I hoped my words wouldn't sound too preachy.

"I'm already starting to see," he said, his smile becoming slightly more intense than I was expecting. I took advantage of hearing a kicking sound coming from the barn and quickly turned my head to pretend I was looking at where the sound was coming from. Not very sly, I know. But I didn't know what else to do. Edward and I weren't exactly on the same page. At least I didn't think we were.

"I better get checking on the ponies," I said. To my surprise he bent down and gave me a hug and then said goodnight. I walked away feeling like I had accomplished something but yet I was still totally confused on the decision I had to make. It was definitely a good night to call home and talk it out. That would definitely make me feel better.

I stopped at the bathroom on the way back to our bedroom to wash up and get ready for bed. I had just gotten off the office phone with my sister and told her everything that Sven and Ms. Arnot had offered. As impressed as she was she told me that my responsibility was back at home and that she would eventually need my help again with the everyday chores back in Ohio. She was right. But I wasn't so sure that was the right answer.

I mentally made a pros and cons list in my head. So far, they were both tied. Not helping.

When I got back to the room I was practically attacked by Gertrude. She was ready to explode as soon as I walked in the door.

"Where have you been?" she demanded. Wow, I didn't realize she cared so much about my whereabouts. Now thinking about it, I guess it is weird for me to leave the barn for no reason. I'm like a faithful barn cat. I always hang around because I know what's good for me.

"I went for a walk in the woods. Why, what's wrong?" I asked, ever so slightly concerned.

"Well, nothing's wrong, I guess," she started. I could see that foggy look in her eyes as if she had something really important to say but once she thought about it, it wasn't so important anymore. Haven't we all been there before.

I dug under my pillow, took out my pajamas and started changing. I was mentally exhausted from thinking so hard that night that I really didn't need to hear whatever gossip Gertrude had to share. As a matter of fact, I was almost going to tell her to save it until morning but that might hurt her feelings. After all, she had helped me an awful lot that past weekend getting Indie ready so I did owe it to her to listen to her story.

I continued to pull the sheets back from my bed and started to crawl in, still waiting for Gertrude to let loose on me. I glanced over at her and saw her texting away on her phone. I guess that news was super important.

"So," she took me by surprise when she threw her phone down on her bed. "Did you hear what was going on?"

Obviously not.

"It's Edward. He's moving out to California to manage Sven's barn!"

Holy Shitake mushrooms.

Chapter Sixteen

How am I supposed to make my decision now? I didn't want the fact that Edward would be there to sway my thoughts one way or the other. He went both on my pro and con list.

We still had six weeks left there at the farm which made me wonder how much longer Edward was planning on staying. Did he know that I was offered a riding position with Sven? Should I tell him? Oh, this was compounding my dilemma even more now. I didn't get a whole lot of sleep the night before and my dreams were extremely active, leaving me even more tired than I should have been that morning.

Sven was leaving the next day and I still hadn't come up with any questions to ask him. At lunch I decided I would start brainstorming the important things I would need to know to help with my decision. My brain felt like it was on overload and I didn't know where to start unloading and organizing the information. For the moment, I had to concentrate on the job at hand. I was still Ms. Arnot's student for the rest of the summer regardless.

Ms. Arnot broke my train of thought when she poked her head into the stall I was cleaning.

"Dana, you will be riding with Sven again today if that is okay with you."

Duh. I mean, "That would be great! What time does he want us ready?"

"He expects you in the arena at noon."

"Okay, thanks!" And off she went. Great. That doesn't leave me a lunch time to brainstorm! I decided to run back to the room to grab a piece of paper and a pen to keep in my pocket just in case I was struck with some sort of wise question.

On the way back to my stalls I started getting somewhere with my thoughts. Number one on the list: please explain the financial aspect again because it just doesn't add up to me.

Number two: how do I get Indie there? I'm sure I'll think of some better questions to put between number one and number two but it was a start for now.

****

Indie was brilliant during out lesson. I took it as a good sign that we would work very well with Sven in California. More than likely I was just trying harder than usual but hey, if that's the motivation it takes to push me forward, I'll take it.

I felt funny asking Sven questions about his offer out there in the open since no one really knew what was happening yet, so I asked if he could spare a few minutes later that evening so I could talk with him. He happily agreed.

We were all invited to a lesson later on that afternoon to watch Sven work his magic on Rinaldi. It would be exciting to see if he could make the fascinating horse any more fantastic. Arthur and Gertrude still had not been offered a ride on the magnificent beast and I felt kind of bad. For Gertrude of course. I had lost respect for Arthur several weeks before.

Speaking of Arthur, he had certainly made himself very sparse lately. The chummy buddies he had been with Gertrude were all but a distant memory. She and I hung out together and I was okay with being her mentor so to speak. But Arthur had become very distant, and I would not have put it past him if he were to pick up and leave one day without warning.

I knew it would be fine with me if he did. It was almost as if he didn't feel obligated to make a good impression and learn from Ms. Arnot anymore. I didn't know what happened to him but I knew it was the least of my worries. I could also tell that it took everything in Ms. Arnot not to blow up at him. I wasn't sure why she wouldn't though.

We had our regular rides on the school horses in the afternoon. I had pretty much taken over the seven-year-old which had proved to be a great help with my riding skills for Indie. Gertrude and Arthur had switched horses a few times but now had their own "regulars" to ride as well.

It was a nice routine we had all fallen into. I still cleaned Arthur's two extra stalls but now I realized Ms. Arnot wasn't trying to punish me. She just wanted her horses well taken care of and apparently she realized soon enough that Arthur wasn't going to be that reliable. I take it as a compliment now, although back then I wondered what she had against me.

The three of us gathered in the viewing room to watch Sven ride. Just as his ride was getting started Gertrude asked out loud, "So, have you talked to Edward yet?" Mortified, I scrambled to think of something to say before Arthur felt the need to enter the conversation.

"Um, no. But I've been a little busy this morning so I'll find him later. No biggie." At least I tried to play it off as no big deal, for Arthur's benefit.

But I felt it. I felt Arthur's gaze slowly turn toward me with a questioning look. I didn't even have to see his face to know what was coming next. A barrage of questions that were, quite frankly, none of his business.

"Edward seems to be a pretty popular topic among the two of you. Do tell," he started.

"There's nothing to tell, Arty," I said, hopefully distracting him with my nickname fetish.

"Then why do you need to talk to him?"

Shoot. It didn't work. I looked over at Gertrude and gave her my don't-you-dare-say-anything looks. I think she actually understood what I was not saying.

"It's no big deal, really." I so wanted to throw in some witty, sarcastic comment but decided that would probably just egg him on more.

We continued to watch in silence for the next few minutes until the unthinkable happened. No, I take that back. Anything is thinkable in my world. Edward walked into the viewing area. Instantly, Arthur pounced.

"So what's up with you and Dana?" Arthur asked. Edward looked confused and slightly terrified at the question.

"Um," he started, throwing his glance in my direction. I just dropped my head into my hands and reprimanded Arthur like he was one of my first graders.

"Arthur," I said sternly as I looked up from my irritated position. "There is nothing going on. I had some barn-related questions to ask him and haven't had the opportunity to ask yet. There. You happy now?"

"Fine," he said in his whiny little voice.

"O..K..," Edward added. "I guess I came at the wrong time."

"No, you're fine. Stay and watch with us for a bit if you can," Gertrude invited. Annoyed at everyone now, I kept my attention at the ride taking place in the arena, ready to go out there and sit alone without the constant questioning and glares from the others.

We finished watching the ride in peace and before it was over Arthur was out the door and in the arena, ready to grab Rinaldi and do his best at sucking up to Sven. He had heard what had happened over the weekend with me and Sven but was still unaware, as was Gertrude, of the opportunity that had been offered.

Little did Arthur know that his efforts were going completely to waste. He lost his opportunity, if there ever was one for him, by lacking discipline and responsibility in front of two Olympic riders the previous weekend.

Gertrude was heading out as well so I took advantage of the brief alone time with Edward. Keeping my voice low I decided I needed to know his side of the story. I walked over to where he was standing, his warm and inviting smile drawing me closer, but not too close. I knew better. I didn't know a gentle way to approach the topic so I just dove right in and asked.

"So, Gertrude informed me that you are moving to California to work with Sven. True?" Instantly, the smile turned to a look of shock. I cringed, knowing I had struck a nerve.

"I'm so sorry. I should have warned you before I pounced," I quickly tried to soften the blow that had already been struck. I wondered if he would be mad at me for being nosy.

"No, that's totally a fair question," was his reply. He ran a hand through his sandy, rough hair and walked over to the couch and sat down.

Uh-oh. Was this going to be a long conversation? Because I still had work to do. Besides, now that Gertrude had been keeping tabs on me I was sure she would be charging back in there shortly, looking for me and demanding a reason for my tardiness. I decided not to sit but I did lean against the wall directly across from him.

"Remember in the woods yesterday," he paused. Oh boy do

I remember the woods yesterday. For more than one reason, but that's not where we're going right now, so focus. I nodded my reply.

"I, too, have a decision to make. Yes, Sven asked me to come out and manage his barn. But no one knows yet."

"Um, correction. If Gertrude knows, everyone knows. I'm sure she's telling Arthur as we speak."

"Oh, right. Well, I haven't made any definite decisions yet but it really is an awesome opportunity. This gig here was just temporary anyway. My previous job was outsourced and I had been looking for work for five months before my aunt asked me to help out here for the summer. But that's all this is. A summer job. This work with Sven would be permanent."

"Sounds great. So what's the problem?" I asked, not quite seeing the issue. He looked up at me and simply shook his head before dropping his gaze back to the floor.

"Things are complicated, with family and stuff."

That was such a typical guy answer. Stuff. Meaning, I don't want to share my feelings and don't want you to see me weak so I'm just going to keep it all clammed up inside. Fine, be that way. Apparently it was nothing I could help him with because I didn't know the family stuff he was dealing with at the moment.

"Well," I started as I pushed myself off the wall. "Maybe a little prayer might help."

"Ha!" he laughed out loud. "And how has that been working for you so far?" I didn't like his cynical tone but I shook it off and took advantage of the fact that he had been listening and remembered what I had said the night before.

"I don't know yet because I can't get past listening to myself yet." I could see the questioning in his eyes but he didn't speak. So I continued. "My heart is torn for several reasons and I keep finding myself trying to choose which way to go, forgetting that it's not really my choice. I have this thing with patience … I don't really have any."

"I've kind of noticed," was his dry reply. I opened my mouth to say some snide comment but I decided turning a new leaf and keeping my opinions to myself was something I wanted to bring home from this trip.

"I've gotta get back to work. I'll catch up with you later." I threw a friendly punch at his left arm before heading out the door. I wanted to get to my alone time so I could think clearly and hopefully come to some conclusions about what I was supposed to do about my invitation to California.

****

Wednesday morning came too quickly. Sven had come to the barn to say his goodbyes to all of us and I felt I owed him an answer even though I wasn't 100 percent sure about my decision yet. I still have a few more weeks here with Ms. Arnot regardless of the final decision I make about whether to go to California or to go home.

I had spent most of the night praying for an answer and coming up with the same result over and over in my head and heart. But I wasn't sure if it was what I wanted or if it was truly what God wanted. What I want and what God wants is a fuzzy line when it comes down to it. My overactive imagination tends to have conversations with itself without me sometimes, and I'm not always sure if it is God talking or just the consistent chatter in my head.

Sven was walking through the barn, saying goodbye to the horses and to Gertrude and Arthur. I stayed back for a bit, wanting not to make my goodbye all that public. After all, I still hadn't made a big deal to anybody about what Sven had offered. I had mentioned it to Gertrude just in passing the night before. She seemed to be happy for me but we really didn't talk about it so I wasn't completely sure if she understood the entire concept. Maybe that's for the better.

I realized, as I stood there waiting to say my goodbyes, that my underarms and palms had suddenly decided it was time to let the flood waters go. Why was I so nervous? I was glad Edward was nowhere in sight. I didn't need any influencing in my decision and he certainly was a major factor when it came down to my final answer.

Laughter suddenly brought me back to earth and I saw Sven and Ms. Arnot make their way toward me. Oh Lord, let me be making the right decision.

"It was so nice to have been introduced to you this weekend. I've really enjoyed working with you and your Indie," Sven started.

"Thank you. And thank you for taking the time out of your busy schedule to work with us. I really appreciate everything you've done for us."

"You have quite the lovely gelding. I hope you have taken some time to think about my offer. Do you have any more questions?"

Okay, Dana. Here it goes.

"I'm sure there are a hundred questions I need to be asking you, but right now I think the only question is going to be how do I get Indie to California?" Silly, but I felt a tear start to well up in my eye. Great. Once that dam broke there was no going back.

Sven's smile was so big that I thought his skin was going to stretch right off his face. He leaned forward and gave me a huge hug which made the tears multiply and start to sneak out of my tear ducts. Curse my oversensitivity.

After a round of hugs from Ms. Arnot as well Sven handed me his card with all his contact information and informed me that Ms. Arnot would help coordinate schedules and shipping. I felt like a kid at Christmas. It was like opening the biggest present but not knowing what it was or how it worked.

We said our goodbyes and I ran to the bathroom to have some alone time to let what I just did sink in for the first time after saying it out loud. I couldn't stop smiling. I was so excited to know that I was starting a new chapter in my life. It is going to be such a dramatic lifestyle change for me but I am totally up for the challenge.

I was quickly brought to tears again when I realized I wouldn't be going home from Canada. I would be shipping out directly from Ms. Arnot's stable and I almost couldn't handle the fact that it would be a long time until I saw my family again.

I also had to let the fact that I just essentially quit my job sink in as well. I loved teaching but I did start late in life, so the fact that I would be retiring when I was seventy was another reason to quit now. Really, how often do you get invited to ride with an Olympian? If I wait until I retire then I won't have the great horse that I have now. Will there ever be another Indie in my life? I didn't want to wait and find out.

I'm going to California.

Chapter Seventeen

Needless to say, my parents and sister were not real happy with me right then. I knew deep down they would see the plus side of the situation but at that point it was a bit hard for all of us to swallow. I couldn't get any sleep the night before because my mind wouldn't shut off. I started to make a pros and cons list in my head and hoped, again, that I had made the right decision. It felt right but uncertainty and doubt of what I was getting into was constantly weighing on me.

But doubt leads to worry and in my book worrying is a sin. God would not have opened the door if He didn't feel I was ready to enter down a new path. Well, technically He can do whatever He wants, but I like to think the just are rewarded for their good works. Maybe this is my reward for staying true and righteous on the path during my stay here in Canada.

Arthur has officially stopped talking to me which doesn't bother me in the least. It does give me even more motivation to work harder at the farm these last few weeks. I know how Ms. Arnot felt about Arthur at the beginning but I'm pretty sure she has changed her thinking.

Annabella was one the first to come and congratulate me on my upcoming trip to California. She seemed genuinely happy for me and I felt a sudden connection with her that I didn't feel before. It's almost like I earned her approval. I was happy for that.

Gertrude took it better than I had thought. She wanted me

to start signing things just in case I became famous. I told her she would be the first one in line for an autograph should things go the way she hoped. I'm not seeking fame, though. I am seeking to fulfill my purpose here on earth. Some people do great deeds and heal people. Others are prophetic. Me, I can ride. But I will do my best and do it for the glory of the Lord.

Working in the barn that morning gave me a refreshed look on life. How awesome our God is when we just wait and listen. Being away from home really gave me the opportunity to rely on Him more than I would have perhaps if I were still doing the same old same old back home that summer. Don't get me wrong. I absolutely love my barn and our business but when you get into such a routine you start to forget how to become dependent on the One who is actually looking out for your future.

I've seen that dependency here and I don't want to lose that feeling. California is going to be a lot tougher than my life here. Not only the atmosphere itself but the people as well. I have a feeling I am going to have to develop a thick outer shell in order to not let the things of this world get me down. Of course, everything is always easier said than done. Man, I am going to be in for a shock.

****

I had just stepped out of the bathroom after a nice long, cleansing shower that evening when I saw a tall figure in the shadows. I gasped and froze, heart pounding out of my chest until I realized it was Edward. Was it me or was he starting to become a bit of a creeper? I mean really, who waits outside a bathroom door, on more than one occasion for a person to emerge?

"What is your problem?!" I practically shouted. "Are you trying to scare me to death?"

Oh great. Was that hurt or concern I saw on his face? "Sorry," I quickly apologized realizing that he must have something important to say if he had taken the time to wait outside my door until I was done.

"Gertrude told me you were showering but I needed to catch you tonight," he explained.

"Oh, okay." It was a bit awkward standing in the aisle with my clothes balled up in my arms, hoping that my underwear wouldn't fall to the ground in front of him. "Do you want to come in?" I asked, nodding toward the room.

"Sure. Here, let me get the door for you."

Here comes his gentlemanly charm. I was really starting to hope that Gertrude would be in the room to give me some moral support. I glanced around our tiny room quickly and was relieved to find her reading a magazine at the kitchen table. I walked over to my bed and threw my dirty balled up clothes under the covers to avoid any wardrobe malfunctions.

Edward walked over to the table where Gertrude was sitting and picked up a magazine off the table, obviously assuming they had to deal with horses. I didn't have time nor did I want to warn Edward before picking up one of Gertrude's addictions.

"Hmph," was his only response before tossing the magazine back on to the table.

"What was that for?" Gertrude asked, looking not the least bit distressed over his disapproving grunt. "If you don't like it don't read it."

Curious as to which ones she was reading that day I walked over to the table and picked up the same magazine. I couldn't help but laugh out loud as I tossed it back on the table as well.

"Oh come on Edward. Everyone likes some good body art

once in a while."

"I didn't peg you for the *Tattoo Daily* type." He stared at Gertrude for a moment, almost as if he were contemplating asking her if she had any tattoos, before he shook his head and looked at me, hoping I would redirect the conversation. I just smiled, raking my hands through my wet hair, enjoying the temporary uncomfortable feeling he was having.

But I could see his discomfort turning to something else, perhaps more caring and gentle and my smile quickly became a nervous twitch. Gertrude apparently saw it, too, and quickly picked up her magazines and made a beeline for the door.

"I'll be back in a little bit, make that a lot bit later." I stared at her in panic just as she closed the door behind her. I was feeling uncomfortable.

"Have a seat," I said, pointing to the table as I walked back over to my bed, pretending to get something out of my bag. I searched until I finally found a clip and then took my time trying to get a good chunk of my bangs out of my face. Once I had time to catch my breath I turned back around and walked to the fridge.

"I don't really drink anything but water, but there are some iced teas left if you would like one of those," I offered.

"I'm fine, thanks."

Yeah, I know you are so fine. But I'm not. I grabbed a bottled water and debated sitting down at the table or not.

"What's on your mind?" I asked, still not sitting.

He rubbed his chin for a moment before taking in a deep breath. Oh, for the love of horses, just spit it out already, I wanted to shout.

"I talked to Sven," he finally said. Okay, not such a big deal. We all talked to Sven at some point during his trip and we both had big decisions to make. As much as I wanted to I hadn't told him that I had made the decision to go to California yet.

"After milling it around, with all the pros and cons, I made my decision about the barn manager position that Sven offered me in California." He paused and then continued.

"But there is something else I need to talk to you about first."

Uh oh. I wasn't expecting anything else. I quickly sat down and leaned on the table, suddenly very interested in what Edward needed to tell me. The floor was his, the time was now. He cleared his throat before continuing.

"I have a bit of a confession to make and I'm not sure I should be telling you this right now. But I feel I owe it to you. Promise me you'll keep this between us, at least for a while?"

The suspense was literally killing me. I was about to jump across the table and start shaking it out of him. But I politely replied, "sure."

"I'm not exactly who you think I am," he started, looking directly at me. He was searching my face just as much as I was searching his. I didn't feel uncomfortable or mad at him but now I was intrigued to find out why he had been lying to me all along.

"What do you mean?" I asked.

"Well, let's just start with what is true about me." He leaned back in his chair and crossed his arms over his chest. "I grew up around horses even though I never pursued a career with them. I went off to school and became a private investigator. That is what I am. A PI. I have been in management for a while as well, just in a different capacity.

"My work mainly consists of small business investigations, and a lot of insurance fraud in the equine world," he continued.

"Okay …." I drew out the word. "But why not tell me that in the first place?"

"Because I am here on assignment."

Oh, that certainly changes things.

Edward leaned back onto the table as he continued.

"There has been an ongoing investigation through the Federation Equestre Internationale of riders gaining international recognition to further the value of their horses just before creating an accident where the horse needs to be euthanized. They are doing it for the increased insurance money due to the increased value of their horses. It's actually quite long and complicated, really. But the point is ..." he trailed off for a moment. He looked directly into my eyes as he put his hands over mine.

"The point is they sent me here to investigate the Americans that were traveling internationally."

Me? Gertrude? Arthur?

Arthur, definitely Arthur.

"So, what you're saying is that you really aren't a manager but a PI who is investigating the three of us?" I pulled my hands away from his as I sat back in my seat, letting all of it process.

It really wasn't processing at all. It didn't make sense.

"Am I in trouble?" I asked, slapping a hand up to my forehead.

"No," he kindly smiled. "Thankfully, no one is so far."

I gasped remembering the shadowy figure.

"Who was the shadow then?"

"Ah, that was Marcus. He was also assigned to the investigation but apparently needs to work on his stealthy skills. He was only here to drop off some intel for me. Just like the gravel truck driver."

Oh my gosh. I completely forgot about him.

"That jerk works with you?" I asked.

He chuckled. "Technically, yes. He was dropping off an updated security system just in case anything went down. We need-ed the proper equipment."

"So, I'm guessing you're not a creeper then," I said.

"No, not a creeper," he chuckled. "I spent more of my time wandering around the barn and the property than doing any-thing else it seems. You just happened to catch me."

We both sat there for a moment, staring at each other. I still couldn't figure out if I was mad at him, relieved that he told me the truth, or none of the above.

"And then there was Gertrude," he continued, obviously feel-ing obligated to explain his relationship with her.

"Oh no! What did she do?" I asked, shocked that she would have anything to do with this scheme.

"Unfortunately, as an investigator it is my job to get close to the subjects in question. I felt terrible leading her on, that wasn't my intention. I just needed to spend some time with her and, well, she took it the wrong way. But I had to keep her trust, so I continued to find ways to build that trust." He genuinely looked upset about what he had to do. If he had to get close to all of us then there was something I needed to ask him.

"What about me?"

"How about we start with Arthur." He stood up and started pacing the tiny little room.

"Okay."

"Arthur was our main suspect. I had to tail him on the week-ends to see what he was up to. Unfortunately, I got to see a side of him that I would rather not relive. He is an odd character in his personal life, but delving further into his background proved he was here for other reasons. He is actually being questioned as we speak."

What? I couldn't believe this was happening. Here, under my

nose. The whole time. All I could do was sit there, mouth open, brain spinning. I knew Arthur was questionable.

"I know this is a lot to take in and I apologize. But I wanted, needed you to know." There were those kind eyes again. Edward took the seat next to me and took my hand, seeing the confusion on my face. He was thoughtful and patiently waited for me to regain some reality. After a moment of processing I was able to speak.

"Did Ms. Arnot know the whole time?" I asked.

"Yes, she was approached before you guys even came up here. She gladly agreed to help out in any way she could."

"So continue. I do believe we are up to me now," I reminded. I was on pins and needles waiting to hear what I had to do with all of this.

"You are the reason I am telling you all of this without the investigation being completely closed. There are still red flags but for the most part you and Gertrude are definitely in the clear. The investigation will continue with other riders being the center of attention. Unfortunately, there are others."

"I'm still needing clarification. You said I am the reason. Why?"

He looked down at our clasped hands, searching for the right words to say. I know that trick. I do it myself.

Looking up he added, "I was afraid to get close to you. I knew you were clean but it was my job, and I didn't want to pretend around you."

Ouch. Was he pretending the whole time that he cared? The hurt was more than visible in my face and I knew it, and I didn't even try to cover it up.

"Dana, listen," he said, scooting his chair closer. I stiffened under his touch and proximity but remained still.

"I called in to be taken off of this case officially. I didn't want to risk our friendship over some ridiculous investigation. I care for you. I don't want to lose that."

I could tell what he was saying was the truth although my head told me not to believe a word out of his mouth. After all, that is his job. To deceive people so they trust him and bare their soul to him.

But I still wanted to trust him and bare my soul to him. It wasn't worth the fight or the argument of what happened in the past. But it was definitely worth the risk.

"I believe you," I whispered, cautious not to let any emotions take over.

"You do?" he questioned, taken aback by my faith in him.

I laughed at his surprise and then stood up. He followed by standing up as well.

"Thank you for telling me the truth," I said as I leaned in and gave him a hug.

"No, thank you for believing me." His voice was full of relief as we broke our embrace.

"So," he started, holding both of my hands in his. "I hear you and I are going to be working together again."

"What do you mean?" I asked.

He smiled and let out a brief laugh.

"Guess who's going to be your new manager in California, Polar Bear."

Epilogue

"Everything looks good," Gertrude called out from the tack room. I had just finished packing all of my stuff in the horse trailer that was going to be hauling Indie to California. I was a nervous wreck and sick to my stomach with excitement. Gertrude was kind enough to double check everything for me, just in case I left something behind.

I can't believe the day is actually here for us to be heading to our new home. These past few weeks have literally flown by and I feel almost unprepared to leave. Almost.

We have grown so much as a team, Indie and I, just over these last three months that I can't wait to see what we will become over the next year under Sven's training. That's what I'm giving it. I'm giving myself a year to see what becomes of my horse career before making any more life-changing decisions. One life-altering change a year is all I can take right now.

"Thanks," I hollered back. I had all my personal stuff packed up in my little blue car, realizing I was going to need to do some shopping once I arrived at my final destination. That was the least of my worries.

Edward had already flown out to Sven's to start his managerial routine. I was thankful that I would see a familiar face once I arrived, and I knew he would help me get adjusted to our new surroundings. I was grateful we had our talk and that he was able to tell me the truth. We had grown to be very good friends and I was so thankful to have met him on my journey.

As for Arthur, well, he never made it back to Ms. Arnot's stables. He was sent back to the United States and put on suspension for a year pending further investigations. It was sad, really, but I'm glad he was caught.

I was also looking forward to seeing my family again. It's been a long summer and I have missed them more than anyone could imagine. They have decided to take a family vacation to California for a week to spend time with me and do a little sightseeing. I know my sister can't wait to see Edward.

Neither can I.

30261917R00106

Made in the USA
Middletown, DE
19 March 2016